"I know you're in there! Open this here door!"

Longarm halted. He did not recognize the voice, but he recognized the tone. Reaching under his coat, he clasped the grips of his double-action .44-40 Colt and withdrew it from his cross-draw rig. Then he moved to one side of the door and flattened himself against the wall.

"Don't let him in, Custis!" cried a familiar female voice. "He's got a gun! He'll kill you!"

This second voice belonged to Widow Davis—Mrs. Constance Davis, to be more exact. It was Widow Davis's bed, in fact, that Longarm had warmed this past night.

"Come on! Open this door, damn you!" cried the irate male. "I know you're in there!"

"Maybe if you huff and you puff you might be able to blow the door in!" Longarm goaded. He smiled. The door was not locked . . .

TABOR EVANS

LONGARM

AND THE
BLIND MAN'S VENGEANCE

A JOVE BOOK

LONGARM AND THE BLIND MAN'S VENGEANCE

A Jove Book/published by arrangement with
the author

PRINTING HISTORY
Jove edition/December 1984

ISBN: 0-515-06273-1

Jove books are published by The Berkley Publishing Group,
200 Madison Avenue, New York, N.Y. 10016. The words
"A JOVE BOOK" and the "J" with sunburst are trademarks
belonging to Jove Publications, Inc.

PRINTED IN THE UNITED STATES OF AMERICA

LONGARM

AND THE BLIND MAN'S VENGEANCE

Chapter 1

Standing fully dressed before the open window of his room, Longarm stared moodily down at the streets of Denver. He could smell it again—that persistent, mysterious smell of burning leaves. Where it came from he had never been able to find out. And here it was the middle of a sweltering July.

There were other confections to jolly the nose as well, creating a noisome stew that Longarm was not all that anxious to inhale every morning. It was compounded of coal smoke, woodsmoke, and the well-pounded essence of horse manure, the fly-encrusted remains of which littered the streets and gutters and alleys of this bustling mile-high metropolis.

Longarm's lean face cracked into an ironic smile

1

as he saw the direction his thoughts were taking. He was getting restless again. It was time to shake these crowded streets, the stuffed shirts, and the pot bellies. And above all, it was time to pull free of the coiling arms and devouring lips of all the widow women who seemed so bent on roping a free man. Why was it, he asked himself, that these women always insisted that Longarm "needed" them, implying that without their fussy ministrations, he wouldn't be able to button his own fly.

Longarm turned away from the window. He was a big man, lean and muscular, with the body of a young athlete. There was little that was young in his face, however. Seamed and lined, it was cured to a saddle-leather brown by the razor-sharp winds and the unrelenting suns of countless distant trails. His eyes were gunmetal blue, his hair the color of aged tobacco leaf. The ends of his mustache he kept meticulously greased, and he liked to think that it gave his appearance a certain unpredictable ferocity. There were times when a man in his line of work needed this.

During the previous night, he had not slept in an empty bed, and in the hour before dawn had returned to his room to freshen up. His hasty toilet now complete, he glanced in his mirror, checked his mustache, then took his snuff-brown Stetson off the bed and positioned it carefully on his head—dead center, tilted slightly forward, cavalry style. He was wearing a brown tweed suit, with a black string tie knotted at his throat. His cordovan leather boots were low-heeled army issue.

With a swift, catlike tread, he started for the door, his tall figure seeming to loom in the small, low-ceilinged room.

"All right, Long!" cried a harsh, masculine voice from the other side of the door. "I know you're in there! Open this here door!"

Longarm halted. He did not recognize the voice, but he recognized the tone. Reaching under his coat, he clasped the grips of his double-action .44-40 Colt and withdrew it from his cross-draw rig. Then he moved to one side of the door and flattened himself against the wall.

"Don't let him in, Custis!" cried a familiar female voice. "He's got a gun! He'll kill you!"

This second voice belonged to Widow Davis—Mrs. Constance Davis, to be more exact. A week before in the Windsor Hotel, she had approached him as he was passing through the lobby and asked him if he would advise her on the mysteries of the gaming table. Her saucy green eyes and full bodice had prompted him to oblige. It was Widow Davis's bed, in fact, that Longarm had warmed this past night.

"Come on! Open this door, damn you!" cried the irate male. "I know you're in there, you son of a bitch!"

"Maybe if you huff and you puff you might be able to blow the door in!" Longarm goaded. He smiled. The door was not locked.

A boot was brought up heavily against the door. The door splintered but did not give. Then Longarm heard as well as felt through the wall a scuffle on the other side of the door and a short nip of pain, followed by the unpleasant sound of a woman's soft body falling to the floor of the corridor. In a moment, Longarm realized, his landlady would be up the stairs wanting to know what in blazes was going on—and he did not want her to run into this fellow. She might get hurt.

He reached over with his left hand and yanked the door open. A big, swarthy fellow was bent over Connie Davis. Glimpsing Longarm in the open doorway, Connie screamed out a warning. The fellow spun around, bringing his revolver up as he did so. Striding out swiftly, Longarm knocked the gun from his hand with the barrel of his Colt. As the fellow's sixgun struck the floor, Longarm brought his Colt back up and caught the man on the side of his face. The sound of unyielding metal crunching into bone filled the narrow hallway. Rocking sideways, the big man slammed back into the wall, then slid slowly down it to the floor, his eyes vacant.

Longarm helped Connie to her feet. He really did not have to ask the question, but he did anyway. "Who the hell *is* this man?"

"Pete, my husband."

"I thought you were a widow."

"I am—or I was. It was my first husband who died. This one hangs on like a summer cold."

Longarm walked over and looked down at the unconscious cuckold. He was big enough to hunt bears with a switch. His shoulders were as wide as a barn door. Maybe he could have huffed and puffed and blown Longarm's door in, after all.

"What's he do for a living?"

"He's a teamster. I hadn't expected him back from Tucson so soon."

He looked at her. In addition to a fresh bloody gash on her forehead, Connie had a purple welt which nearly covered one side of her face. She had been worked over pretty thoroughly even before she got here. It had certainly taken courage on her part to follow her husband in order to warn Longarm.

"Don't mind how I look," Connie told Longarm. "It was my fault for getting caught."

"That's right, Connie. Now let me give you a piece of advice. Leave this fellow. He's mean enough to kill, and it looks like he's already made a start on it."

"Does that mean that you and me . . . ?"

"Nope. Don't mean nothing like that at all."

"But, Custis, I know you like being with me."

"And that's the pure truth of it, Connie. We get along fine, sure enough, and you do know how to welcome a man to bed. But let me say it right now and get it over with: I'd just never be able to trust you, Connie."

Connie lowered her head. She was a foot shorter than Longarm, with reddish auburn hair, soft eyes, and a round, babyish face. She was not slim or bony, but full and ripe and lush. The extra meat on her bones hadn't slowed her down any, and he had had a little trouble at first keeping up with her.

5

"I guess I deserve that," she said, her voice low.

"But you don't deserve to get your head stove in when this wild man comes to his senses. Do what I told you. Leave him. Divorce him, or whatever."

"He won't let me. He said he'd kill me if I tried to leave him."

"He'll kill you if you don't."

She looked up at Longarm for a full minute, then glanced over at her still unconscious husband, considering Longarm's warning. "All right," she said, her expression reflecting sudden resolve. "I'll do it. I'll go back to my place, gather my things, and leave Denver. My pa's got a ranch up north. Do me good to get out of this ant heap."

"My sentiments exactly, Connie."

Connie flung her arms around Longarm's neck and kissed him full on the lips, her mouth working hungrily. Then she pulled away.

"I'm glad I met you Custis Long," she said. She turned and went down the stairs.

Longarm walked over to Pete and waited. The right side of his face was already swelling from Longarm's blow. The big fellow opened his eyes. Longarm hunkered down in front of the man, smiled, and rammed the muzzle of his Colt into Pete's mouth.

"This here's to get your attention," Longarm explained reasonably. "Have I got it?"

Pete, his eyes narrowing in fury, nodded.

"Good. I am not going to see your good wife again. She told me she was a widow, but that's neither here nor there. The thing is, if I hear of you hurting her

6

in any way, I'll come after you and knock that thick skull of yours so far down between your legs you'll be wearing your balls for earrings. Is that clear?"

Again Pete barely nodded his head. He was in pain and he knew that Longarm was capable of delivering on any promises he made, but his eyes remained cold and defiant. There was something exceedingly savage and unforgiving prowling behind those eyes. For a moment, Longarm wondered if this man wasn't part Indian. He thought of Connie then and decided he better give her a little more time to clear out.

He pulled the muzzle of his revolver out of Pete's mouth and rang the top of his noggin with it, hard. Pete Davis's eyes rolled back into his head. He uttered a sound like a horse makes when you take off its saddle, then settled loosely onto the floor.

"Tarnation!" cried Billy Vail, shaking his head in exasperation. "You know I can't have one of my law officers going around smashing up local citizens. Especially over a married woman!"

Slumped in the red leather easy chair by Vail's desk, Longarm glanced idly at the burning tip of his cheroot and waited for the United States marshal to simmer down.

"I didn't know she was married, Billy."

"Would it have made any difference?" he barked.

Longarm thought a moment, then shrugged. "I guess not. She was a pleasure to be with, and that's a fact."

"Another thing! If that husband of hers had a weapon and threatened you, you should have had him arrested and pressed charges. Now all you've done is commit assault and battery and then left the man free to try again!"

"There's one solution, Billy."

"Oh?" Vail's bushy eyebrow cocked angrily.

"Get me the hell out of this town."

Vail leaned back in his seat and appraised Longarm coldly. His cheeks were pink and his head was balding, but he didn't look comical at the moment, and Longarm wondered if maybe he hadn't said the wrong thing just then. Only God knew what kind of awful assignments flew in from Washington to land on Vail's desk.

Then Vail smiled. It was satanic. He leaned forward in his chair and rested his elbows on the blizzard of paper on his desk.

"I got just the job for you, Longarm. It'll take you way the hell up into Utah Territory. How's that grab you? Should sure as hell be far enough from these here fleshpots."

"Go on."

"You ever hear of the Mullin Gang?"

"Who hasn't?"

"I mean lately."

"They disbanded, I hear. The Pinkertons kept after them something fierce. There was talk they fled to South America, Mexico, some say Canada."

"Washington does not like to have a private detective agency outshine the U. S. marshal's office. You can understand that, can't you, Longarm?"

"I reckon so."

"I have a wire here from Washington. Been sitting on it for a week now. It seems one of the gang members has returned to his home in Dun Creek and is willing to testify against the other members of the gang—to reveal their present whereabouts, which stages, banks, and trains they robbed. It is a real neat package he's offering. All any prosecutor would need to lock that gang up for keeps."

"What's his name?"

"That's the problem. We don't know which one it is."

"Make sense, Billy."

Vail poked around among the debris on his desk, then hauled forth the letter he was looking for. As he handed it to Longarm, he explained, "This letter came from Washington yesterday. It's the reason for that cable last week. Washington sent it along to me by mail so I could have a look at it. What's in this letter is all we got to go on."

Longarm took the letter from Vail, unfolded it, and read it over quickly.

Dear Sirs:

I am writing this letter to inform you of my desire to turn myself in. I am a member of the Mullin Gang. But I am sick and tired of hiding out and being hounded by the Pinkertons. I will give myself up and tell you all about the gang and where you can find them. Also I will tell you which banks, trains, and stagecoaches we robbed.

But I will not talk to anyone unless I am assured that, for my cooperation, I will be treated fairly by the federal prosecutor. You can reply to this letter by writing to P. O. Box 21, Dun Creek, Utah. Address the letter to Box Holder.

Sincerely,

A member of the Mullin Gang

When he finished reading it, Longarm glanced up to see Vail watching him carefully.

"Well," Vail asked, "what do you think?"

Longarm shrugged. "This fellow sure don't sound like a member of a gang of outlaws—less'n he's gone to college since."

"My own thoughts precisely. What else?"

"This is a woman's handwriting."

Vail's eyes lit in agreement. "How can you tell?"

"This is the way my schoolteacher used to write on the blackboard. The letters in each word beautifully formed, the flow, the neatness. It's just plain beautiful to read. No man ever wrote this."

"And certainly not a member of Mullin's gang, as high-flying and thievin' a band of rascals and cutthroats as ever held up a stage or stopped a train."

"So the whole thing is a hoax, you think?"

"That's what I think, and so does Washington. What do *you* think?"

Longarm leaned back and took a long drag on his cheroot, frowning thoughtfully. He glanced down at the letter again, read it over, then leaned forward and dropped it onto the desk in front of Vail.

"I think it might be a trick, but I don't think you can risk not checking it out."

"Exactly. If this is on the level and the Pinkertons get a similar letter, follow it up, and come up with the Mullin Gang, it's bound to come out that we screwed up."

"Which means you got no choice."

Vail nodded. "We're going to have to check it out."

"And I'm the one you want to send."

"You said it was time for you to shake Denver, and after this morning's fracas, I suggest you be on the afternoon train. I'll see to your travel vouchers. You pack your gear."

Longarm stood up and took his hat off the corner of Vail's desk. "Then let me have that letter. It might come in handy."

Vail got up and handed Longarm the letter. "Don't lose it. It's the only lead we've got."

"I'll be back in a couple of hours with my gear," Longarm told Vail, pausing before the door. "If I'm not, just figure another irate husband found me."

Vail waved Longarm out the door.

"Bromfield, next stop!"

The conductor's sharp cry aroused Longarm to a sitting position. As the conductor slammed out of the day coach on his way to the next one, Longarm shook his head and glanced out the window. He had dozed off some time ago and, judging from the position of the sun in the sky, it was now late afternoon, which meant the train was on time.

Longarm shook his head to clear the tentacles of sleep that still clung to him, then ran his big hand across his face and readjusted his hat. The train was lifting into high country now, and the welcome splash of green pine on the hills above the tracks gave Longarm some comfort after so many miles of scrub and desert land.

Unfolding his cramped legs, he rose and stretched to ease the kinks. Then he swung his carpetbag down from the rack and carried it through the swaying coach onto the platform between the cars. The wind held a strong spicy scent of sage and sun-warmed pine. The train whistled as it neared the station. The screeching brake shoes began to grab and hold. Longarm set down his carpetbag and braced himself with a hand on the railing.

The first shacks of Bromfield slid past, then an empty loading corral for cattle, after that a switch. Wheels rattled over rail ends. Windows flashed the lowering sun back at him. The whistle sounded again and the bell began to clang. The train eased up along the cindered apron fronting the station, slowed to a crawl, then halted with a final grinding lurch.

Longarm stepped down. The solid ground underfoot felt strange. It had been a long ride from Denver and the brief stopover in Salt Lake City had only depressed him. Straight streets, straight men and women, and straight faces everywhere. A smile would crack those Mormons in two, he reckoned.

He walked over cinders to the baggage car, retrieved his Winchester, then continued on to the wooden platform. A man went by him pushing a baggage truck. Longarm walked over to the depot, set his carpetbag down on the platform, and leaned his rifle against the building.

He looked back at the train, watching the brakeman hurrying by, tapping carriage wheels while the engine panted and hissed clouds of steam, as if infuriated by this halt. Farther along, the door to a freight car was slid open, and three men began unloading boxes and crates.

Longarm watched all this, but he hardly saw it. He was trying to decide on his next step. He was still about fifty miles from Dun Creek, and since there were no army posts nearby, he would have to rent a mount from the local livery stable. But it was late, and he was looking for an excuse to stay in Bromfield overnight. Then he could start off fresh in the morning.

He was still pondering his options when a familiar figure got off the last coach on the train and hurried across the cinders toward the station platform. Her bruised face was heavily powdered and the single suitcase she was lugging was so unmanageable that she apparently did not see him.

He snatched up his carpetbag and rifle and moved to intercept her. "Want some help with that, Connie?"

She hauled up, squinting in the glare from the westering sun. "Custis! What are you doing here?"

"I was about to ask you the same thing."

She let the suitcase slam to the platform. "Now, if you're thinking I was following you . . . !"

13

"Wasn't thinkin' anything of the kind. Here, let me give you a hand with that suitcase. You've just helped me make up my mind. I was looking for an excuse to stay here overnight."

"If you're sure I'm not imposing..."

"You know better than that. Here, take this rifle, and we'll go find a hack."

They found one on the other side of the depot. Longarm lifted Connie's suitcase and his carpetbag up onto the baggage rack on top of the hack and told the driver to take them to the best hotel. The driver told them there was only one.

"It'll have to do," said Longarm, and leaned back in the seat.

"This is too pleasant a surprise to be a coincidence," Connie remarked. "Someone up there is looking after me, I'm thinkin'."

"Why do you say that?"

She rested her head on his shoulder. "I'm tired and lonely and running from a madman. And then you turn up. I feel better already."

"Is that ranch of your father's close by here?"

She nodded. "The Lazy H is about twenty miles north of Dun Creek. My pa is Clem Hardin."

"Does he know you're coming?"

"He will when I get there."

"I'm on official business, Connie, so the most I can do is ride with you as far as Dun Creek."

"Who says I'm ridin' with you?"

Longarm shrugged. "I just thought..."

"There's a stage goes through there in two or three days. I'll just wait here for it."

"Suit yourself."

"I've no wish to be riding that far on horseback and sleeping on the ground under the cold stars. It would ruin my curls."

"And we wouldn't want that."

"No, we wouldn't."

They pulled up at the hotel. Longarm got out first, helped Connie down, then paid the driver after the fellow lifted down their baggage. As the hack rattled off, Longarm glanced up at the hotel. It was a graceless hulk of a building, a story taller than the other buildings crowding Main Street. Leading the way, Longarm carried Connie's suitcase and his own carpetbag up the porch steps and into the musty-smelling lobby. Connie trailed in after him with his Winchester.

He signed the register and turned to Connie. With a shrug, she signed it also. The clerk did not bother to look at the names as he handed Longarm a key. Then he called for a bellboy. An ancient cowpoke with bowed legs appeared and preceded them up the stairs to their room on the third floor. He opened the door for them, raised a window, then planted himself at the foot of the bed with his hand outstretched.

Longarm gave him a quarter. The old man's eyes lit up and he almost did a jig as he swept out of the room and closed the door. Longarm looked around. The room was certainly big enough. It had one large double bed. Two porcelain pitchers and washbowls

15

sat on the commode, with fresh linen and towels folded neatly beside them. Longarm tested the mattress.

Connie looked at him. "If this is against your principles, Custis..."

"It ain't. I figure you've lit out, so that makes it all right. If you was an Indian, that's all it would take, you know. You'd just go back to your mother's people and you would no longer be bound to that brave."

She frowned. "Funny you should say that."

"What do you mean?"

"My husband is part Indian."

"Which side?"

"His father's."

"What's his Indian name?" Longarm asked.

"Little Bear."

"How come you're Mrs. Davis?"

"That's my first husband's name. After Pete married me, he took my last name for his and called himself Pete Davis. That made it easier for him to get by as a white man. When he was known as Pete Little Bear, everyone was always trying to goad him into a fight."

"You think maybe that's why he married you? To get your last name?"

She shrugged. "Sometimes I wonder."

"I'm going downstairs to find a barber. I need a shave and a bath. I'll meet you in the dining room about five. How's that?"

"Sounds very nice, Custis."

He smiled, picked up his carpetbag, and left the room.

● ● ●

Longarm took his bath first, reveling in the suds and the pails of steaming hot water the attendant poured over him. He could have spent the evening in that big steel tub, but his stomach told him it was steak time. As he clambered out, the attendant, a young lad of sixteen, hurried over with a bath towel and handed it to Longarm.

Longarm thanked him and began rubbing himself down vigorously. The kid remained at Longarm's side, evidently troubled by something. Longarm dried off his hair and smiled down at the kid.

"What is it, kid? You waitin' for your tip?"

"No, sir."

Longarm handed him the towel. "Then what is it?"

"You got any enemies in this town, mister?"

"Not that I know of. I ain't been through here before."

The kid took a deep breath and nodded. "I didn't think you had."

Longarm finished putting on the fresh longjohns he had taken from his carpetbag, then reached for his shirt. "So why did you ask me that, kid?"

"A mean-lookin' feller wanted me to heat the water to boiling and then dump it on you. He offered me ten dollars if I would."

Longarm finished buttoning the fly on his britches. Stepping into his boots, he looked closely at the kid. "What'd this gent look like?"

The boy paused a moment, then described Constance Davis's husband. Finishing up, the kid remarked

17

that he looked as crazy mean as an Indian.

Buckling on his cross-draw rig, Longarm shrugged into his frock coat and stuffed his string tie into a side pocket. Then he put his hat on and took the boy by the shoulders. "Which way did he go when he left here?"

"Across the street."

"To that saloon?"

"No, the hotel."

Snatching up his carpetbag, Longarm pressed a double eagle into the kid's hand and strode swiftly through the barbershop and across the street. He was thinking of only one thing as he started up the hotel steps. He had left Connie up there alone, and it wouldn't take long for this crazed Indian to find out which room Connie was in.

Approaching the desk, he couldn't find the desk clerk. He called out for assistance and a somewhat shaken desk clerk appeared from the office.

"Yes, sir?"

"Has anyone been here inquiring about Connie Davis?"

"Yes, sir," he replied, shivering. "A most violent man. He slapped me."

"Did you tell him which room she was in?"

"Of course. He said he was her husband."

Longarm took the steps two at a time. As he started for the second landing, he heard a muffled shot. He was racing down the corridor to his room when the door opened. Pete Davis appeared in the doorway, a huge Walker Colt in his hand. He aimed quickly at

Longarm and fired. The detonation shook the flimsy walls and the slug took out a chunk of plaster beside Longarm's head. Longarm flung himself flat and drew his own Colt.

Davis turned and ran. Longarm aimed carefully and fired. The shot shattered a window beyond Davis just as he vanished around a corner. Longarm leaped to his feet and gave chase. At the end of the hall, he charged through a door and came out onto an outside stairway. Davis had already reached the alley floor and was leaping onto his horse, a big chestnut. Longarm pulled up and aimed, but before he could get the shot off, Davis had vanished up the alley.

Holstering his gun, Longarm raced back to his room. There was a crowd gathering in the corridor outside it by this time, all of the curious staring into his room. Longarm barged past them, slammed the door shut on them, and looked for Connie.

She was on the floor on the other side of the bed, lying in a pool of her own blood.

He winced when he saw her, then bent and picked her up and placed her on the bed. What her husband had started on her face before, this time he had finished. And there was a neat black hole just under her left breast.

Connie opened her green eyes. "I was such a fool," she whispered. "I should have known he'd be on that train, following me."

"Don't talk. I'll get a doctor."

She reached out and grabbed his arm. "No, stay! I'm going to die. I know it."

19

"Don't talk silly."

"Please! Listen to me. Will you see to it that I get back home to pa's ranch? Tell him to bury me near ma, on that little hill back of the orchard. He'll know the spot. I talked to him about it once."

Longarm swallowed and nodded. Connie's voice now was barely above a whisper and her complexion was gray.

"You said you could never trust me, Longarm."

"That was cruel."

"But it was the truth. And I understand. But, do you think, Longarm, that maybe after a while you might have trusted me?"

Longarm smiled and stroked back her hair. "Yes," he lied. "Of course I would."

Connie smiled. Her breathing came in short, gasping breaths. Longarm leaned close to tell her he was going for a doctor. As he did so, he saw the light in her eyes go out. Her head fell to one side. Longarm got to his feet, went around to the foot of the bed, and looked down at her.

She had been so pleased to see him. To her it meant she would now be safe—and, as she put it, someone up there was looking after her. Jesus, had she ever been wrong.

Chapter 2

"God damn it, Randy," Longarm muttered, "keep low!"

Longarm shifted the rifle in his hand, then crouched down behind the rock, his eyes on the old cowpoke's figure standing beside the campfire in the arroyo below. The wagon carrying the pine coffin was a dim, barely distinguishable shape squatting just out of the reach of the fire's flickering light.

Longarm had given the old bellhop specific instructions. He had told him not to stop at all, but to continue on to Dun Creek through the night without pause. Longarm was almost certain Pete Davis would make an attempt to get him, and this coffin on its way to Dun Creek was a perfect lure.

Longarm had driven the wagon out of Bromfield in plain sight that night, and met Randy Walls outside of town. Longarm's hope was that Davis would not know until too late that he was not driving the wagon— and, by that time, Longarm would have the drop on him. Astride the black he had rented at the livery stable, Longarm had kept to the timber above the stage road, his eyes never leaving the wagon, waiting and hoping for Pete Davis to make his move.

But, as Longarm might have figured, the old man had grown weary and had pulled off the road to camp in this arroyo only ten or fifteen miles from Dun Creek.

Longarm decided to move closer. Pulling back off the ridge, he circled around behind the draw, then came out above a crowd of boulders halfway down the slope. His long frame bent low, he angled down toward them. From their cover he hoped to gain a better view of Randy and the campfire and the pine-covered slope behind it. He was anxious to see to it that no harm came to Randy Walls. He had already endangered the old cowpoke enough by hiring him to take Connie's coffin to Dun Creek. If Pete Davis made his move from those pines above Randy's camp, Longarm was confident now that he would have a clear shot at him.

Slipping in among the hulking boulders, Longarm flicked off the safety catch on his Winchester. He had already cranked a fresh cartridge into the firing chamber. Then he peered over a hip-high boulder at the camp below. Randy was tucking himself into his soogan, the light from the dying campfire flickering over his huddled form.

Too late, Longarm heard the shift of a pebble underfoot. He spun and saw something sweeping down out of the night toward him. He started to duck, then felt the gun barrel crack him a glancing blow on the side of his skull. His hat went flying and he staggered back against the face of another boulder. His brain reeling from the blow, he felt himself sinking to his knees. With a cold, pleased grin on his dark face, Davis clubbed Longarm again, then stepped closer and brought up his Colt a third time. He would rather beat Longarm's skull to a pulp, it seemed, than finish him off with a clean bullet.

Dropping his Winchester, Longarm flung up both arms to ward off the next blow. As the Winchester struck the ground it detonated, but Davis paid no attention and continued to bore in on Longarm, bringing his Colt down again and again on the lawman's skull in a series of mean chopping blows that sent sharp daggers of pain shooting through his head. Longarm fought him off with less and less efficiency, his senses now reeling drunkenly. As if he were standing off at a great distance, he saw himself groping blindly out at his attacker in a desperate, futile attempt to wrest the punishing gun from his grasp.

A shot came from behind Longarm. He saw Davis's hat fly off. The man glanced up in surprise, then snatched his hat off the ground, turned, and scrambled back up the slope toward the ridge. Another shot came from behind Longarm. Tiny shards of stone leaped up from a boulder just ahead of the fleeing Davis. Longarm sat down suddenly, his back slamming into a boulder, as he continued to stare up at the dim, fleeing figure outlined for a moment against the starlit sky before it slipped over the ridge.

A hand grabbed Longarm's shoulder. Longarm saw the seamed face of Randy Walls peering down at him.

"Looks like that son of a bitch done beat your brains to a pulp, mister," Randy said. "You sure as hell outsmarted yerself this time." The old man leaned his ear against Longarm's chest. Frowning, he looked back into Longarm's face. "Damn," he whispered. "Yer a gone beaver!"

By this time, Longarm was dimly aware of the hot tentacles of fresh blood streaming down over his face. Desperate to communicate to Randy, he struggled to speak, to tell the old man he was conscious—that he wasn't dead, damn it! But his lips refused to move.

"Can you hear me, mister?" Randy asked, his voice soft with melancholy. Reaching out, he shook Longarm's shoulder gently.

When there was no response, Randy shook his head regretfully. "All right then, Mr. Long, I'll just move out before that son of a bitch comes back. Don't worry. I'll get this here body to Dun Creek, like you wanted."

The old cowpoke appeared reluctant to leave, but he stood up with a regretful sigh.

Longarm watched helplessly as the man bent to pick up the lawman's rifle, then vanished into the darkness. For a moment Longarm heard him scrambling down the slope to his campsite. Exerting himself to the utmost, Longarm struggled to get to his feet. But all he succeeded in doing was pushing his back an inch or so away from the boulder he had been lodged against. Slowly, inexorably, like an old barn giving way under a heavy load of snow, he sagged slowly over onto his side.

Stella paused in the doorway. She was certain of it this time. A horse was nickering softly, anxiously from somewhere in back of the carriage barn, and that was not where the horses were. They were in the front corral, unless Abe had moved them for some reason.

She turned about in the doorway and faced the bunkhouse. "Abe!" she called.

A wiry old man as straight as a hoe handle with alert blue eyes and a thick thatch of snowy white hair emerged from the bunkhouse. "Yes, Miss Stella?"

"Where's the stock?"

"In the front corral, where you said, Miss Stella."

She nodded and turned back into the kitchen. Placing the dish she'd used to carry the chicken feed down on the counter, she brushed her long auburn hair off her forehead and walked through the kitchen to the bedroom.

For a moment she stood looking down at the sleeping form of her husband. Then she bent and shook him by the shoulder.

"Bob, get up!"

He opened his eyes and gazed at her. "What's the matter?" Last night's whiskey laced his breath.

"I can hear a strange horse out back. Someone's out there."

"Go see for yourself," he said, rolling over and pulling the covers over his shoulder.

She straightened and looked down at the balding, disheveled head of the man she had married too quickly and for all the wrong reasons. Well, she'd made her bed. Turning angrily, she left the bedroom, walked back through the kitchen, and went out the door.

Abe was in the act of lugging a full bucket of water from the well to the bunkhouse. For a moment she considered calling him, then decided against it, and continued around back and headed for the main barn. There was no horse in sight as she approached the big open doors. She felt a little silly.

Then she heard the nicker again, louder now and unmistakably impatient, coming from behind the barn. She hurried past the open door and cut through a small tangle of alders. A black was tethered to a sapling at the edge of the stand. Moving closer to it, Stella spoke softly, attempting to soothe the animal. His eyes were wild, his nostrils flaring.

"Easy, boy," she said, moving to him and taking hold of the reins. "Easy now. That's the feller."

The horse was still saddled, a bedroll neatly packed behind it, a large carpetbag descending from leather straps on one side. The rifle scabbard was empty. The horse's legs were gray with sweat-hardened dust and he had cropped all the grass within reach. She felt the horse's nose. He needed water. That was why he had been complaining.

But whose horse *was* this? And where was the rider?

She looked back at the barn and remembered its wide-open doors. Hurrying back through the alders, she stepped into the barn's cool interior. She moved cautiously around a buckboard which Bob had let slip beyond repair, then started looking into the stalls. Most of them were piled high with loose hay.

She was moving past the fourth stall when she caught a furtive movement out of the corner of her eye and whirled to confront a tall stranger leaning upright in one corner of it. In the dim light provided by the single dirt-encrusted window behind the stall, she could see that the man's head had been fearfully beaten. Horrible dried tentacles of blood reached down his face all the way to his neck. He wore no hat and his thick shock of hair was encrusted with blood.

"Who . . . who are you?" she gasped. "What do you want?"

As soon as she spoke, the man pushed himself out of the corner and groped feebly toward her. Stella's hand flew up to her mouth involuntarily and she took a step back.

"Name's Long, Miss. Custis Long. And right now I'm looking for a place where I can maybe put my head back together."

"Oh, yes! I can see! You've been hurt! Hurt bad!"

she said. "Are you on the run from the law?"

He shook his head slightly. The effort seemed to hurt him terribly, and he rocked on his feet. "No, I ain't, ma'am. I was trying to make it to the ranch house last night, but only got this far."

As he spoke, he started to slump. She saw his knees buckle. Swiftly, she stepped closer, braced herself, and caught him. But he was such a tall, powerful man, that she was forced to let him down easily onto the stall floor, as his dead weight threatened to crush her beneath him. As soon as he was resting on the floor, she straightened up and stepped back, her heart racing.

Then she became aware of the heavy slick of fresh blood that bathed the front of her dress all the way down to her knees. With a shriek, she whirled and darted from the barn, her near-hysterical cries bringing Abe on the run. The old man caught her halfway between the barn and the ranch house and shook the hysteria out of her, then led her into the kitchen, sat her down firmly at the table, and went into the bedroom to rouse her husband.

By the time the two men had managed to carry the stranger into the ranch house, Stella had changed her dress and readied the bed her husband had just quit. She was furious with herself for her hysteria of a moment before and was now in firm control of herself. Abe was carrying the stranger by the legs, Bob by the shoulders, and as Abe backed into the bedroom, he looked questioningly at Stella, obviously reluctant to deposit the blood-sodden stranger in her bed.

"Go ahead," Stella told Abe firmly. "Put him down."

"Yes, Miss Stella," he said, swinging around so that the beaten man's legs would rest at the foot of the bed.

"Christ, Stella!" Bob complained hopelessly, as soon as he had dropped the blood-caked head onto the pillow. "Where are we goin' to sleep now?"

"You can sleep in the bunkhouse with Abe. "I'll sleep on the davenport in the sitting room. But, for now, I think you had better ride into Dun Creek for Doc Gilmore."

Bob Loman looked distastefully down at the cruelly battered figure. "He'll be dead before I get back," he said, looking back at Stella.

"Perhaps."

"I don't see why we should bother about him. Who is he, anyway? Just some drifter that got himself beat up."

"If you want, Miss Stella," said Abe, "I'll ride in for the doc."

Stella looked at Bob. "Will you go, please? I need Abe here."

Her husband considered a moment. Then his pale eyes lit craftily as he considered the ride to Dun Creek to hunt up Doc Gilmore. It didn't need to be such an unpleasant chore, at that.

Stella saw the gleam in his eye and understood at once. "Just don't you and the doc get liquored up," she told her husband.

"Or you'll what?"

In a low, firm voice that cut like cold steel, she told her husband, "Or I'll see to it that this time you *stay* in the bunkhouse."

Loman made a feeble effort to square his shoulders. "Now, see here, Stella! That ain't no way for you to talk to..."

But Stella had already turned and was on her way back into the kitchen, Abe following obediently after her. Loman caught himself, glanced down in frustration at the long stranger bleeding in his bed, then cursed and reached for his hat.

Bob Loman reached Dun Creek a little past noon, a sullen ghost of a rider as dry as the dust that clung to him and his horse. As he prepared to dismount before Steadman's saloon, he noticed a small crowd in front of the funeral parlor.

"What's up?" he asked a cowpoke who was whittling a stick on the saloon porch.

"Some old codger brought in a coffin this morning. Seems like it's Clem Hardin's daughter. He just rode in to get it."

Loman shrugged and continued on down the street until he came to Frank Warren's barbershop. He stuck his head in the door. Warren was lathering a customer's face.

"Frank, the doc back there?"

"Nope. Ain't been here all morning."

"Well, if he comes by, you tell him I want to see him. I'll be in Steadman's."

"Reckon since you asked me nice and proper, I'll

be glad to do that," the barber said, turning his attention back to his customer.

Relieved that he had not been able to locate the doctor immediately, Loman turned back around and hastened back to the saloon. The clink of poker chips coming from a table at the far end of the place was the only sound besides that of his spurs as he bellied up to the bar. Big Jim Steadman was behind the bar this early in the day. He nodded curtly when he saw Loman.

"Whiskey," Loman said.

Steadman waited for Loman to slap a coin down on the polished mahogany before he reached back for the bottle and poured Loman's drink. *Thanks, you son of a bitch,* Loman muttered under his breath as he drew the shotglass carefully up to his lips.

Steadman waited until Loman placed the empty glass down on the bar. Then he smiled thinly at Loman and said, "You're welcome, you son of a bitch."

Loman frowned in surprise. He hadn't realized the saloon owner had heard him. "Didn't mean nothing, Jim," he said. "Just seems like you'd know by now I'm good for it."

"Sure, Mr. Loman, I understand. You're a big rancher now."

Loman kept his temper and pushed his glass toward Steadman for a refill. "The doc been in yet?"

With his thumb Steadman indicated a table in the back. Loman glanced over and saw the doctor slumped forward onto his arms. Sheriff Gulch was playing poker with a big, dark man at the next table.

"The doc's sleepin' off his breakfast," Steadman said. "You'll have a little trouble waking him up, I'm thinking."

"Thanks," Loman said, tossing down the whiskey.

As Loman approached the sheriff's table, the fellow playing poker with the sheriff glanced up at Loman and fixed him with cold, unblinking eyes. They were as dark as an Indian's and lit with an unholy light. The fellow was big and rangy, with hair the color of a raven's wing. He was a hard case, all right. Loman had never seen the man in town before, and he wondered if Paxman could possibly be thinking of another raise. If so, it was the first Loman had heard of it.

"Hi, Gulch," Loman said.

"Ain't you startin' early, Loman?"

"I ain't stayin'. Stella sent me in to get the doc."

"You mean she's in a family way so soon?"

Loman felt his face color, but he kept his head and didn't let himself get exercised. "She found some guy in the barn, got himself beat up pretty bad. Now the poor bastard is bleeding all over our bed."

The fellow playing cards with the sheriff looked with sudden intentness up at Loman and tossed in his hand.

"That so?" the sheriff said. "What happened to him?"

"Beats the hell out of me. But it looks like someone tried to plow his skull with an axe. He won't be alive when I get back with the doc, but you know how Stella is."

"Hell," said the sheriff, grinning, "I don't know how Stella is. Unless maybe you're inviting me to go find out."

"You ain't got no call to say a thing like that, Gulch!"

"Sure, I have. I got a right to say anything I damn please to Bob Loman. This here layoff has turned you into a loose-mouthed lush. You ain't no good now to Paxman or anyone else. And I'll bet you ain't no good even for that woman you married."

Loman went for the sheriff. But the big fellow with Gulch stood up swiftly, reached out, and grabbed Loman by his shirt. Pulling him close as easily as if Loman was some kid's rag doll, he shook Loman hard for a minute to get his attention.

"All right, mister," he said to Loman. "Now what about this feller at your place? Is he big?"

Loman pulled himself anxiously back from his interrogator. He was confused, glad he had been prevented from tangling physically with the sheriff, but furious at the ease with which this big guy hauled him around. "Yeah," he managed. "That's right. He's big."

"Longhorn mustache, brown hair, brown suit?"

"Yeah. You know him?" Loman asked.

"No."

Gulch interrupted sharply. "Go wake up the doc, Loman. Get him out of here. He's stinkin' up the place."

Loman moved hastily around the table, tried halfheartedly to shake the doc awake, then gave up and left the saloon. The hell with that big stranger

33

Stella was so eager to help. It didn't matter to him if the bastard lived or died.

Loman headed across the street to the livery. He'd split a bottle with Hoss before going back to the Bar S. Maybe two bottles.

As he crossed the street, he seethed with resentment at the way Sheriff Gulch and that big son of a bitch with him had treated him. Didn't they have no respect? Didn't they know who he was? He was one of the original members of the Mullin Gang!

Inside the saloon, Pete Davis shook his head when the sheriff asked him if he wanted to play another game.

"What's the matter?" Gulch asked. "Did I clean you out already?"

"Nope. That ain't why I'm quittin'." Then Davis fixed the sheriff with his cold eyes and waited.

"Okay," Gulch said. "Spell it out."

"I know who that gent at Loman's place is."

The sheriff put down the deck and leaned back in his chair. "Go on."

"He's Custis Long. A federal marshal."

The sheriff came alive at once. Leaning closer, he said, "You sure of that, Pete?"

"I'm sure."

"What in blazes is he doin' up here?"

Pete Davis shrugged. "I could tell you, but it would be none of your business."

"Just answer me straight. Does this U.S. marshal know who Paxman is?"

"I don't know. All I know is, he's a federal marshal, and he's up here looking for someone."

Sheriff Gulch leaned back in his chair and looked Pete over with sudden renewed interest. He was remembering something he had heard one of the express messengers talking about this morning after their run up from Bromfield. "How do you know all this about that feller?"

"Like I said before, it's a private matter. You can believe me or not. That's your affair."

"Hell, I got no reason not to believe you." Gulch leaned forward. "But I think Paxman better know about this. I think I'll ride out now and tell him."

"I'll go with you."

"Yeah. Maybe you'd better, Pete. Paxman'll want to know all about this here federal marshal."

The two men got up quickly and strode from the saloon.

Jim Mullin, the man who now called himself Jim Paxman, sat facing the open window, his face lifted to catch the full wash of the bright sunlight. He could feel its warmth slanting across his seamed face, down his vest, and over his left forearm. He liked to sit in the sun like this, drinking in the smells that came in the open window, especially the pungent odor that came from the sun-baked grease on the axles of the spring wagon just outside the window.

From the way the sound carried and the feel of the sunlight on his face, Mullin had little trouble imagining the sky's cobalt blue and the white glare of the

35

hard-packed front yard before the main corral. But it was his ears that brought the yard to life for him: the lazy shuffle of his cowpokes as they went about their business, the nervous hooves of the broncs circling inside the corral—while above it all rang the steady clangor of the blacksmith's hammer from across the compound. The sound of that steady, solid, ringing beat brought to his mind's eye a picture of the bright white flame guttering in the bellows' blast and the rippling muscles of his giant of a blacksmith as the man brought down his hammer. . . .

Breaking suddenly into this mental image came the drumbeat of hooves as two riders rode through the gate and up to the ranch house. He heard their horses blowing as the riders reined in. When they dismounted, he heard the chink of each man's spurs, followed by the hollow clumping of their boots crossing the verandah.

As his housekeeper answered their knock and let them in, Mullin swung his swivel chair around, pulled it up behind his desk, and directed his dead eyes at the door. A few seconds later it swung open and he heard the two men stride into his office.

Not until the housekeeper pulled the door shut behind them did Mullin acknowledge their presence.

"Well, who is it?" he demanded sharply.

"It's me, Gulch."

"And who's that with you?"

"An old partner of mine, Jim, from Tucson. Name's Pete Little Bear."

"My name's Pete Davis now, Mr. Paxman."

"Sounds like you're a big man, Pete."

"He's big enough, Jim," broke in Gulch. "He's been spending the last couple of years raisin' stages all by his lonesome." He chuckled. "Even his wife didn't know."

"Oh? What did you tell her, Pete?"

"That I was a teamster."

Mullin chuckled and turned his blind eyes toward Pete. "A man with real talent. But as you can see, Pete, things have slowed down some for me and the rest of my boys since these here lamps went out."

"Sorry to see that, Mr. Mullin."

"Get in the habit of calling me Paxman," Mullin said quickly.

"Sorry, Mr. Paxman."

"Just don't do it again." Mullin smiled bleakly. "Meanwhile, stick around. Gulch and I have been planning a raise. We might deal you in if you're willin'. We need another rider."

"I'd consider that a privilege, Mr. Paxman."

Mullin smiled and leaned back in his chair. "Fine. Gulch here will introduce you to my foreman."

Gulch cleared his throat nervously. "Jim, that ain't why we rode out here."

"Oh?"

"There's a federal marshal at Loman's ranch."

Mullin frowned. "What did you say?"

"You heard it right the first time. Loman just rode into Dun Creek looking for Doc Gilmore. This marshal showed up at his ranch with his head stove in. According to Loman, he might not live."

"What in hell's he doin' at Loman's ranch?"

"I don't know, Jim," the sheriff said.

"How can you be sure he's a federal marshal?" asked the blind man.

"Pete knows him."

Pete spoke up then. "He's a federal marshal, all right," he said. "I met him in Denver, then I saw him in Bromfield when he got off the train."

"But how do you know that the man you saw in Bromfield is the same one who turned up at Bob Loman's ranch?"

"Loman described him to us in the saloon," Gulch said.

Mullin didn't like it. As always, he knew when he was not being told everything. Gulch was not holding anything back, but this new hand, Pete Davis, was. Mullin could sense that Davis knew more than he was letting on. Nevertheless, Mullin trusted him.

And he believed him.

Mullin turned his face toward Pete Davis. "I appreciate your coming forward like this, Pete. From now on, you're working for the Diamond T."

"Much obliged, Mr. Paxman."

Mullin looked back at Gulch. "All right, Gulch, I'll check into it. This marshal may be here on other business. We've covered our tracks pretty damn well, I'd say. And with you wearing that star, I don't see we have all that much to worry about. After you get Pete settled, tell Benton I want to see him."

"Okay, Jim."

Mullin waited until the two men left his office

before he leaned back in his chair and took a deep breath. He had spoken bravely enough to Gulch and that new hand, but he had a feeling about this—a bad feeling. He reached a hand up to his eyes and drew his palm harshly over the eyelids, as if his hand could work the sight back into them.

A stray bullet from a half-crazed bank clerk had done this to him. What had been at first only a long flesh wound over his eyebrows had become with incredible, devastating speed a festering wound that invaded both sockets. Before the pus-filled abscess was finally drained and cleaned out by a Denver surgeon, his sight had been taken from him. The nerves threading light from his eyes to his brain had been completely destroyed.

Fortunately, the spoils from that last bank raise had been enough for him to buy this ranch and to carry him these past four years. He supposed he could possibly make it as an honest rancher, but he believed a man should do what he did best.

And robbing banks and trains was what he did best, not punching cows.

The Mullin Gang was not through yet. Blind though he might be, his experience would guide his men. He would see through their eyes. Already he was able to ride as well as any man. All he needed was another rider to stick close and warn him of any obstacles ahead.

Pulling open the second drawer on his right, he lifted from it his well-oiled Colt, leaving the holster and cartridge belt in the drawer. Placing the Colt carefully down on the top of the desk, he fitted his hand almost lovingly around the grips. The gun was loaded. He could tell that easily enough from its weight. For a long moment he sat at the desk, the sixgun in his hand, drawing from its solid weight a comforting surge of strength and purpose. Then, with a thin smile on his face, he placed the Colt carefully back into the holster and closed the drawer.

Like a blind spider hidden in the corner of his web, he would wait for this federal marshal to be brought to him—if, indeed, it was Mullin he was after. Then this Colt in his drawer would prove that, blind though he was, this old spider still had a bite. . . .

Through the open window behind him, Mullin heard his foreman mount the verandah steps and enter the house. The foreman's knock sounded a moment later.

"Get in here, Benton!"

Benton pushed the door open, stepped in, and closed it. Then he walked up to Mullin's desk. Mullin could smell the dust on the man and the unwashed feet within his boots. "You want me, boss?"

"I want you to take a ride."

"Where to?"

"Bob Loman's ranch. There's a federal marshal laid up there."

"Jesus, boss! A federal marshal?"

"You heard me. Find out what he knows—why he's in these parts. If he's dead when you get there, just ride back and tell me."

"Okay, boss."

"The thing is, I don't want you to get that woman

40

Loman married suspicious. I don't want her to know why you're there. You got that?"

"Sure."

Mullin waited for his foreman to leave. Instead, Benton shifted his feet and cleared his throat.

"What is it, Benton?"

"If this marshal's at Loman's place, why don't you just ask Loman to check him out?"

"I wouldn't trust Loman as far as I could throw your hoss. Loman's turned into a four-flushing leech, and a lush to boot. It wouldn't surprise me what he'd do to get hold of a bottle. You follow?"

"Sure, boss."

"Then get on with it."

As Benton turned and left the room, Mullin swung his swivel chair around once again and tried to position his face so that it caught the sun. But the sun had gone down already. What he felt instead was a sudden, surprising chill.

It seemed to penetrate to the very marrow of his bones.

Chapter 3

Longarm woke to the sound of a woman's voice. It was coming from behind him, near his head. He opened his eyes and saw nothing. Only gradually did he realize he was staring up at the ceiling of a room. He turned his head slightly and saw a very fine-looking woman, her oval face framed with thick auburn curls, her hazel eyes wide with concern as she leaned close.

She reached out and placed her hand on his forehead, and at once he became aware of how warm he was. A sun was burning inside him, causing an almost intolerable thirst. The woman withdrew her hand as if it had been stung and reached for something behind her. He heard the clink of crockery striking glass, and then the woman was holding a glass of water to his parched lips. The water trickling into his mouth was like nectar. He gulped at it greedily. Some of it went down the wrong way and he coughed, but no matter. He had to have more. He finished the glass and lay back content, his eyes closed, the fire within him momentarily banked.

The woman leaned close. "Can you hear me?" she asked.

He could only open his eyes and turn his head to her.

"Then listen," she continued. "I sent my husband for the doctor this morning. It is past midnight and he hasn't returned yet. Abe here is going to wash off your lacerated scalp with whiskey. It might sting some, but we have to do something. You're going to get an infection if we don't."

From the other side of the bed an older man's voice piped up. "I am going to have to cut some of your hair off, too, mister. But it'll grow back."

Longarm turned his head to face the old man and barely nodded.

As the old man began snipping away at the hair on his skull, the headache that had been dull and remote became more immediate and more angry. He closed his eyes and clenched his teeth and endured. After a while the room receded, even the fiery pain that lashed at his skull as the whiskey was swabbed onto his head, and he drifted off.

The sun was pouring into the room, falling full upon his pillow and the back of his head. Longarm reached up and felt his head. It was swabbed entirely in bandages. And then he realized something else. He could move his arms freely.

But it was not the sun that had awakened him. It was the voices, angry voices. The argument was bitter, intense. It stopped abruptly as the sound came to him of a hand slapping a face. This was followed by the sound of a fist burying itself into a shoulder or stomach and was accompanied by a soft cry of startled pain.

The woman had slapped the man, and he had punched her back.

He lifted his head and turned to look in the direction from which the sounds were coming. The kitchen. Its door was slightly ajar, and the woman was crying now—not piteously, but furiously, with contempt for the man who had struck her and anger at herself for having let him.

"You can get out of here now," she said hotly. "And don't ever come back."

"I'm your husband. You can't kick me out. Remember those papers we signed? I own half this ranch now. I ain't goin' nowhere."

"If you don't go, I'll kill you. I don't know how I'll do it, but I will!"

"Woman talk," the man scoffed. "I should have taken you in hand sooner."

There was the sound of quick movement, a woman's footsteps, and then a man following. The sound of a short, brutal scuffle followed, and then the noise of a heavy cooking utensil falling to the floor. After that the woman cried out, a small, desperate cry this time.

Longarm could almost see the upturned face, the desperation, the helplessness. He sat bolt upright and threw back his covers, disregarding the residue of pain that still stirred deep within his skull. He was wearing someone else's longjohns. He put his hand out and pushed himself toward the kitchen door.

Both of them turned at his entrance and at once Longarm recognized the woman who had found him in the barn and who he now dimly remembered as the woman who had cared for him through so many fitful nights. This man with her was her husband, he realized. But it didn't matter.

He lurched across the kitchen, caught the man about his neck with both hands, and pulled him away from the woman, slamming him violently back against the wall.

The man stayed upright, clawing frantically at his neck and gasping in fury. "You . . . !" he cried. "What do you mean by . . . !"

Longarm said, "You heard her! Get out! Now!"

"Now listen here, you—"

Longarm slapped him across the face, hard. The force of the blow spun the man half around. For a moment he held his face where Longarm had slapped him. Then he backed quickly away toward the bedroom, clawing at his sixgun as he went.

Longarm overtook him before he could get the gun level and swiped downward, knocking the gun from his hand. As it clattered to the floor, the man looked down at it stupidly. Then Longarm punched him on the side of the jaw. He was feeling dizzy now, but half crazy with the delight of venting his fury on this piece of offal before him. He swung again, catching the man on the side of his head this time, causing the fellow's forehead to slam into the edge of a cupboard.

But before Longarm could strike out at him again, he felt a firm hand grasping his right forearm. He turned. The woman was pulling him back. Tears were staining her face, but there was something else on it as well—fear, fear of *him*. Longarm relaxed immediately and pulled back from her husband.

"Please," she pleaded. "You've done enough to him. No more. Please."

Longarm looked back at the man, aware suddenly that he was himself shivering violently. Whether it was from the sudden exertion or the wild, ungovernable fury that had swept over him, he could not tell.

He let his hands fall to his side, then looked back at the woman. "You told him to get out," he said. "And then I heard him hitting you."

"I know," she said weakly. "I know."

At that moment her husband scuttled past Longarm to the door. Once he reached it, he glanced back at his wife. "This won't settle anything, Stella," he cried. "You're actin' crazy! Takin' up with this stranger!"

"Just get out, Bob," she replied wearily. "Please. Just get away from me."

"You're my wife, Stella!"

"You heard her," Longarm said, taking a step toward him. "Get out!"

The man went to the door and opened it. Then, standing in the open doorway, he licked his lips and glared back at Longarm. "I need my weapon!"

Longarm bent, picked up the sixgun, and tossed it to Stella's husband. He holstered it, then looked back miserably at his wife.

"Stella, please! I'm sorry I hit you just now. I...don't know what came over me."

She shook her head firmly. "It's just no good, Bob," she said with finality. "It never was, really. And now...after this... Please just get out of here and leave me alone."

The man's contrite expression vanished instantly. His face darkened with savage fury. "Leave you alone!" he burst out furiously. "You mean leave you with *him!* You think I don't know what's been goin' on behind my back?" He glared wildly over at Longarm. "You ain't foolin' me none! You ain't sick!"

"You will be," Longarm told him softly, "if you don't get out of here."

The man hesitated for only an instant, then stepped out through the open doorway and pulled the door shut behind him. In a moment the quick clatter of his horse's hooves filled the kitchen. As soon as the sounds faded, Stella sank into a kitchen chair beside the table and laid her head down on her arms.

As she wept, Longarm walked over to the stove and the pot of coffee sitting on it. He placed the back of his hand against the side of the pot. It was still pretty warm. Cups were hanging from hooks in the cupboard over the sink. He took down two, filled them with coffee, placed them on the table, and sat down across from Stella.

The smell of the coffee appeared to revive her spirits some. She raised her head and looked across the table at him. She struck Longarm as not pretty so much as handsome, with a fearless, uncompromising honesty in her eyes that he could only admire. Her eyes looked at him now with a deep sadness, and a fear of him that was still there, just below the surface.

"I suppose I should thank you," she said.

"You don't have to if you don't want to."

"He's such a weak man. I was a fool to have married him." She reached out for the coffee and pulled it closer to her across the red-checked linoleum tablecloth. "I thought he would help me run the ranch. After my first husband died, I was so sure I needed help."

"You don't have to tell me anything."

"I know that." She sipped her coffee. "How do you feel?"

"Hungry," he said, smiling. "How long have I been in that bed?"

"More than a week," she said. "You certainly *must* be hungry, at that."

"I could eat a mountain lion, tail and all."

Finishing her coffee, Stella got up from the table and went quickly to the stove. As the kitchen filled with the smell of bacon and eggs frying in the skillet, he watched her cut thick slices of dark bread and drop them into the iron skillet alongside the eggs and bacon. His stomach twisted in anticipation. Just soon enough, she pulled down a huge platter from a shelf above the stove, filled it with the eggs and bacon and bread, and placed it in front of him.

Then she refilled his coffee cup and sat across from him to watch him eat. "Go ahead," she said, smiling. "I've already had breakfast."

He dove in, relishing every morsel.

"How's your head feel?" she asked.

"Hurts some, way inside. But I can live with that. My scalp itches something fierce, but I'm afraid to dig at it."

She smiled. "You hair's a mess. You won't like it. But your scalp's pretty near healed now, and as soon as your hair grows back no one will notice. You'll be as good as new."

"Thanks to you."

"And Abe."

"The old man?" Longarm asked.

"Yes. He's my hired hand."

As he ate, Longarm began remembering. After the old man had cut his hair and washed off his skull with whiskey, Longarm had drifted off into a sleep so deep it seemed more than sleep. And whenever he awoke, it seemed, he would find Stella and the hired man moving about him softly, quietly, their concerned faces bent close. It was her cool hands he had felt on his forehead, her soft voice urging him to lie back down and sleep.

And each time, at her gentle command, he had sunk back onto his pillow and drifted into the deep, delicious sleep that wiped out even the memory of pain, that cooled his raging fever, and quieted finally the thudding torment of a headache that had followed him even into his disordered dreams.

"You haven't told me your name," she said now.

"Long. Custis Long."

"Bob wanted to look through your things, your wallet and the rest of your gear. I wouldn't let him. I've stashed it all under your bed."

"Thank you."

"I'm Stella Loman."

Longarm smiled at her. "I am pleased to meet you, Stella."

Cleaning off his plate with uncommon relish, he finally pushed it from him and leaned back in his chair.

"More coffee?" she asked.

He shook his head and became instantly aware of a sudden, enormous fatigue. It descended on him with a completeness and a finality that astounded him. He looked quickly in the direction of the bedroom and wondered if he would be able to make it back to his bed.

Stella saw at once what had happened. "You're exhausted," she said, getting quickly to her feet and moving around beside him. "Here, let me help you back to bed."

As she helped him to his feet, the kitchen spun violently about him, and his headache returned with a vengeance. He lurched, stumbling, toward the bedroom doorway, Stella barely managing to keep him on his feet. He dimly remembered hitting the bed and her gentle hands pulling the covers up around him.

Mullin could smell the fear and the desperation on Bob Loman as he stood in front of his desk. Fred Benton had escorted him in and was standing at his side. The foreman and Bob Loman really stank up his office. Or was it just that, sightless, he was now leaning more heavily on his other senses, his sense of smell in particular?

"Let me hear that once again, Loman," Mullin said. "Slower this time."

"Stella kicked me out. She's in there with that other guy. He's moved right in on me!"

"How come you didn't fight back?" Mullin asked.

"I did! But that big fellow is too much for me."

Mullin swung his face toward his foreman. "Last time you visited the Bar S, Benton, you came back and told me this guy was still unconscious, his head all wrapped up in bandages."

"That wasn't no lie, boss. Honest."

"Benton was right," Loman explained hastily. "But this here feller, he just appeared in the kitchen doorway and began swiping at me."

"For no reason at all."

"Well..."

"I see." Mullin leaned wearily back in his chair. At once, he saw it all. "Why, you stupid son of a bitch, you were beating on Stella! Ain't that right? And he heard you."

Loman didn't reply, but his silence was all the corroboration Mullin needed.

"Good!" Mullin said emphatically. "Good for that woman! I could tell from the sound of her voice that she had guts."

"What am I going to do, Jim?"

"You got any idea who that big galoot sleeping in your bed is, Loman?"

"No, I don't. I tried to go through his things, but Stella caught me."

"She wouldn't let you, is that it?"

"That's right."

Mullin turned to his foreman. "Get that new hand in here. Pete Davis. Pronto!"

"Sure, boss."

As Benton hurried from the office, Mullin told Loman to sit in a chair along the far wall, as far away as he could. Somewhat mystified by this order—as Mullin could tell from the uncertainty of Loman's steps—Loman complied. Mullin heard him slump into a chair and scrape it back against the wall.

"Now, stay there, Loman, and keep your mouth shut. You follow me?"

"Sure, Jim," Loman responded meekly.

Mullin then turned his swivel chair so that it faced the open window. He leaned back and sucked in the fresh, sage-spiced breeze coming off the flats. A few moments later he heard Benton returning with Davis and swung about to face the door. The two men entered his office without knocking. Mullin heard the door close.

"You there, Davis?" Mullin asked.

"Yes, Mr. Paxman."

"Get closer."

Mullin waited until Davis strode up to his desk. Then he smiled coldly up at him. "Now tell me all about this federal marshal—how you happened to know so much about him, that is."

Davis hesitated.

Mullin moved his head the fraction of an inch, his dead eyes finding his foreman with uncanny accuracy. "Keep your gun on our new hand, Benton," Mullin instructed. "If I don't figure he's telling me the truth, I want you to shoot him."

"No need for that, Mr. Paxman," Davis said anxiously.

"Good. So let's have it. The truth this time."

"I never lied to you."

"You just never told me all you knew about this here marshal, Custis Long. Isn't that right, Davis?"

"That's right, Mr. Paxman."

"Go on."

Davis cleared his throat and told Mullin that Custis Long and he had had a slight misunderstanding over a woman in Denver. When he bumped into him in Bromfield later, they had had another brief altercation, after which Davis had followed Long out of Bromfield, waited his chance, and chopped up his skull with his Colt. Davis thought he had killed him, but the deputy marshal had somehow recovered and turned up at Loman's ranch.

"That's it? That's all of it?" Mullin asked.

"Sure, Mr. Paxman."

"You're lying. I can tell. What's the matter with you, Davis? Don't you want to work for me?"

"Sure I do, Mr. Paxman."

"Who was that woman in Denver?"

Mullin heard Davis shift his feet nervously. "She was my wife."

"That's better. And you followed her to Bromfield and killed her. Is that right?"

"Yes."

"Clem Hardin just buried her, didn't he?"

"Yeah. I didn't know for sure who her folks were until I got up here. But that's her father, all right."

"Good. Now you're beginning to level with me. I'd say it's about time. I own the sheriff in this county, Davis. That means I own the law. Anything that happens in this here territory, I know about first thing. Don't make the mistake of taking me for some no-account gang leader. I'm a power in this territory, a pillar of the community. Go against me and you haven't a chance. But if you're with me, you don't have a thing to worry about."

"Sure, Mr. Paxman."

"Fine. Now, is that all you know about this here deputy marshal?"

"Yes, sir. I told you all I know."

"Then you have no idea what he's doing in these parts?"

"No. But he was with my wife in Bromfield. Maybe he was coming up here to stay with her and her father."

"I consider that highly unlikely, don't you?"

"I was just thinking out loud."

"Save your breath the next time you get the urge, Davis."

"All right," Davis replied, "I'll do that."

Mullin detected a hint of surliness creeping into Pete Davis's voice. The big fellow was doing his best to keep his anger in check. Good. Mullin wouldn't give a pinch of coon shit for a man who would take such a browbeating without resentment.

"Now then," Mullin went on, his voice considerably less abrasive, "as far as you know, Pete, the only reason this deputy U. S. marshal is at the Bar S is because that was as far as he could get, hurt as bad as he was. Is that it?"

"That's right, Mr. Paxman."

Mullin could tell that now, finally, Davis was telling the truth. Mullin knew why Davis had tried to kill this lawman before he had brought him in here. What he had not known, and what he did not know now, was the purpose of the lawman's visit to this territory. He had been hoping Pete Davis might be able to tell him. It was unfortunate that he could not.

"At any rate," Mullin observed, "there's not much of a chance that this U. S. deputy knows who I am."

Mullin's foreman spoke up then. "Hell, boss! How could he?"

"Yes, indeed. How could he?"

"So what are we going to do about him?" the foreman went on.

"I am not sure. But one thing is certain. It would

be better, much better, if he continued on his way to wherever he was going before Pete here stomped on him. I think the best thing is to run Stella off what is now half my property. If we can dislodge her, we should get rid of him at the same time. I just don't like a deputy U. S. marshal sniffing around."

Bob Loman stirred in his chair along the wall. Then he cleared his throat nervously and got hastily to his feet. "Jim, did you say the Bar S was half *your* property?"

Mullin turned his blind eyes on him. "Yes, Loman. You heard right. The Bar S is now half mine."

"But, Jim . . . !"

"Get over here, Bob," Mullin said.

Loman hurried over to the desk.

"Now listen, and listen good, Loman," Mullin told him. "I am going to give you enough gold to get you clear to California. And in appreciation and gratitude, you are going to sign over to me your half of the Bar S."

He could feel Loman straightening up as he considered this deal. He heard the man shift, and in his mind's eye he could see Loman licking his lips. "Well, now, that's real decent of you, Jim. Why, sure!"

"Good. Bunk with us overnight. I'll send for my lawyer tomorrow and we'll draw up the papers."

Then Mullin turned his blind orbs on Davis. "Meanwhile, Pete, keep your hands off this U. S. marshal. I don't want him around here any longer than he has to be."

"I could kill him easy enough."

"Sure you could. Then these hills around here would be swarming with U. S. deputies. I've spent too long building up this ranch and my new identity to see it all blown now. You follow me, Pete?"

"Yes, sir."

"Good. Now get out of here. All of you."

Chapter 4

Longarm sat up, even more ravenous than before, and flipped back the covers. As his bare feet planted themselves on the rough floorboards, Stella appeared in the bedroom doorway.

"How do you feel?" she asked.

"Hungry."

"I've got a steak waiting," she said with a smile. Then she turned quickly back into the kitchen.

"Stella?"

She looked back into the room. "Yes?"

"Where's my clothes?"

"Your shirt and suit are folded on the dresser over there."

"And my holster and sixgun?"

"In with the rest of your gear under the bed—along with that railroad watch, the one with the little gun attached to it. Is it a real weapon, Custis?"

"Is is that. A .44 derringer."

Her eyebrows went up a notch. Then she vanished from the doorway.

When he appeared in the kitchen a few moments later, he was fully dressed. He was pleased with how neatly Stella had pressed his pants and suit. She had even polished his boots. He missed his hat, but outside of that, he felt ready for action once again, even though his pants no longer fit him as snugly as before, and his frock coat hung a mite loose on his shoulders.

He sat down at the table. "How long did I sleep this time?"

Stella put a platter of steak in front of him. "It's the next day," she told him, smiling. "Around four in the afternoon."

He looked down at the steak. It was more than an inch thick and filled the platter. She had smothered it with hot fries, onions, and mushrooms. He set to work on it.

While he was sipping his coffee a little later, they both became aware of the clatter of approaching hoof-beats. A moment later came the sound of hurried footsteps approaching the door. Longarm turned just as Abe opened the kitchen door and poked his head in.

"It's that feller, Benton, again."

"Thanks, Abe," Stella said.

Abe pulled the door shut.

Stella looked at Longarm. "Benton is the Diamond T foreman. Ever since you landed here, he's been riding over. His excuse is that he likes to visit with Bob, but I think it's you he's curious about."

"Did he ask about me?"

"He did."

"What did you tell him?"

"The truth—that you were still unconscious."

"Did he smile at the news?" Longarm was grinning at her now.

"How can you tell if a jackal is smiling or not?" she retorted. "As you'll see, Custis, Benton's a mean sort."

As she spoke, she walked over to the door and stepped out onto the low porch.

Longarm left the table and joined her and Abe on the porch as Benton guided his horse across the compound and reined up in front of the porch. The foreman of the Diamond T was riding a sleek, well-fed stallion. The horse was a sharp contrast to the rider, who was a chunky, slovenly man with bloodless lips and dead-looking eyes set in a pocked face. He wore a collarless shirt and a stained red vest with a Bull Durham tag dangling from the pocket.

He touched the brim of his hat to Stella, but made no effort to dismount.

"Light and set a spell, Benton," said Stella, her voice holding no warmth.

"Can't do that, ma'am," he said.

"Well, what is it you want?" she asked.

"Mr. Paxman sent me over to tell you something."

Benton smiled. It was not a pleasant smile. His uneven teeth were yellowed and broken, like fangs.

"Well, tell it, then," snapped Stella.

Licking his lips, the foreman glanced full at Longarm. "See you're up and about, mister."

"I am."

Benton swung his gaze back to Stella. "Bob was sure put out, ma'am. I mean about you choosin' this gent over him like that."

Stella's face reddened instantly. "How *dare* you!"

"Get on with it, mister!" Longarm barked.

Benton shrugged. "All I know is what Bob told us. Anyway, I came to tell you Mr. Paxman bought Bob's interest in the Bar S. Mr. Paxman thought you might like to know you're his partner now."

"Bob did *what?*"

Benton's horse shifted nervously. Benton reached down and patted his neck, grinning at Stella as he did so. "Yep, ma'am, he surely did what I said. He sold his interest in the Bar S to Mr. Paxman."

"Where's Bob?" Stella demanded.

"On his way to California with the gold Mr. Paxman gave him."

"All right. You've given me the message. Now ride out."

"There's just one more thing. Mr. Paxman is willing to buy you out for fifteen hundred. That's everything, ma'am. Range, stock, barns, ranch house."

"I'm not selling!"

Benton appeared surprised at the response. "That's a good price, ma'am."

"I don't care. I'm not selling the Bar S. And you can tell your boss I'm going to see my lawyer first thing."

"That your last word, ma'am?" Benton asked.

"You hard of hearing?" Longarm asked.

"Nope," Benton replied, looking over at him.

"Then get off her land," Longarm said.

The foreman shrugged, pulled his horse around, then rode out without a single glance back.

Tears of rage and frustration were streaming down her face as Stella went back inside the ranch house. Abe watched her unhappily, then, his hat in his hand, bowed hastily out of the kitchen and pulled the door shut behind him.

As soon as Abe was gone, Stella let go Longarm moved swiftly closer to her and held her tightly, letting her sob it all out. At last she pushed herself away from him, shy all of a sudden.

"I shouldn't let myself get unstuck like that," she said, "but when I think of Bob selling out to Paxman, it makes me so mad!"

"You think your lawyer can help?" Longarm asked.

"Do lawyers ever help?" she asked bleakly. "But I'll go in to town tomorrow and see him anyway. I have . . . other business to tend to as well." She smiled at him suddenly. "You've kept me rather busy this past week."

"I'm sorry about that."

"Don't be, please. I didn't mean it to sound that way."

He smiled. "Now, who is this Paxman?"

"He owns the Diamond T. His land adjoins mine. He's wanted this spread for years."

"A big man in the territory, is he?"

"Big enough. He's also blind—stone blind."

"That's a little unusual, isn't it?"

She nodded. "He went on a trip about four years ago and came back with his eyes infected. Before they could clear up the infection, he lost the sight in both eyes."

"But it hasn't stopped him any," Longarm observed.

"No, it hasn't. He's still land greedy, still running his outfit with an iron hand. Bob worked for Paxman before I married him."

"Stella, I think it's time I moved on out of here. I've already raised hell with your reputation."

"Bob did that, not you."

"Don't make any difference how it happened. Besides, I've got business in Dun Creek. That was where I was headed before I got hurt."

"You haven't told me much about that, Custis."

"No," he said carefully, "I haven't."

"I see. It's none of my business."

"Something like that," he told her gently.

She moved still closer to him. The storm had passed. Her eyes were clear now, and warm. Suddenly she smiled. "I know you must go—and I won't keep you. But it would be such a shame if you went like this."

"A shame? What do you mean?"

"I mean if you left this minute, and I got the name without the game."

By that time her face was inches from his. Raising herself on her tiptoes, she flung her arms around his neck and kissed him firmly on his lips. He understood at once. Chuckling warmly, he lifted her in his arms and carried her into the bedroom.

"About time you got a chance to use this bed again," he told her.

Lying beside her on the bed, Longarm fumbled with her dress and skirts while she peeled off his pants and longjohns with swift, expert fingers. Impatient then, she pushed away his fumbling fingers and released the catches and snaps that held her imprisoned within her dress. Flinging her dress and shift aside, she sat up for a moment and unpinned her curls, sending her long, shimmering tresses cascading down over her shoulders, some of which reached all the way to her full, creamy breasts, where they coiled about her nipples.

He reached up then and pulled her to him. For a few feverish moments they clung fiercely to each other, their naked limbs entwined almost as closely as the strands of a lariat. He kissed her behind her ear, nipped the ear-lobe, then moved his hungry lips to her mouth. She answered his kiss with a passion that astonished him. It was as if she were trying to devour him with her mouth.

"You must wonder at me," she told him huskily, as she pulled her lips away from his finally and began to stroke his bandaged head.

"You're a woman in her prime, Stella. I don't wonder at it none. I just appreciate it."

"Yes, but do let me explain. For the past three months I have been keeping myself from Bob. He stank of whiskey. He was unclean. I used every excuse to keep him from my bed. It was cruel, I suppose, but I could not help myself. I married him because I needed a man, a real man. My previous husband was like a stallion. But this Bob Loman . . ."

"I reckon he was a disappointment."

"Yes."

"I hope I don't disappoint."

She smiled wickedly. "While you were unconscious, I washed you. All of you. All over. At times, you became erect while you slept. I'm not worried about you, Custis."

"Enough talk," he murmured.

"Yes."

She flung her arms about his neck and they kissed again. She moaned as his lips probed hers. Her mouth opened hungrily and, as her tongue found his again, she flung her arms around his neck and ground her naked body up against his. Responding, Longarm brought his hands up to cup her warm breasts. His rough fingertips caressed the nipples. He heard her groan, her arms still about his neck, her tongue still probing with a reckless wantonness that inflamed him. He could smell her. It was the aroma of a woman clean and fresh and aroused, without the taint of soap or perfume. The smell of her filled his nostrils, arousing him to an even keener pitch.

He broke the kiss and took one of her nipples in his mouth. It swelled even larger and grew as hard as a bullet as his tongue flicked it expertly. Stella leaned back, moaning softly, and opened her legs hungrily, arching her pelvis against his throbbing erection. Reaching down, his fingers found the swollen warmth of her pliant lips. Then he reached behind her to thrust her buttocks up as he gently eased his engorged shaft deep into her. He went in as far as he could, aware of the constricting muscles within her grabbing his shaft with the force of a flexing hand.

Stella moaned and flung her head back, brought her legs up, and locked her ankles around the back of his neck.

"Deeper, Custis!" she cried. "Deeper!"

Longarm did his best to oblige. Pulling out, he left just the tip of his erection within her. Then he plunged recklessly into her, driving himself in deeper than he had been able to go before, so tightly had the muscles inside her clutched at him. Then he repeated the thrust, going in still farther the next time. Soon he was driving in with great rhythmical sweeps, plunging deeper and deeper with each stroke.

Stella uttered a sharp, guttural cry that was wrung from the deepest part of her. Her ankles tightened convulsively around his neck as he continued to thrust. "Oh, yes! That's it!" she cried out, in pleasure and pain. "Keep going! Faster! Faster!"

After a dozen or more such thrusts, Longarm felt her juices begin to flow. With each shattering plunge Stella's ecstasy mounted, her cries grew more intense, and it all had its effect on Longarm. He was also moving toward orgasm. He pounded harder, bringing sharp, deep yelps from Stella. Abruptly, she became rigid under him. Her ankles tightened. Her inner muscles squeezed about his erection, and he pressed home, aware of his own pulsing, spasmodic thrusting as he emptied himself within her. She too was climaxing. It lasted for a long, wondrous moment; then they both grew less rigid.

She opened her eyes and looked up at him. Tiny beads of perspiration formed on her forehead. He leaned himself forward onto her glistening body, aware that, miraculously, he was still large within her.

"I can still feel you inside me," she whispered, panting slightly, the tip of her tongue showing through her lips. "They say it's not important—the size of a man, I mean—but don't you believe it, Custis."

He grinned down at her. "I won't if you tell me not to."

With him still inside she rolled them both over until she was on top and—still keeping him inside—hauled both legs up and sat back on his erection, gasping with pleasure as she felt him going in deeper and yet deeper. Soon he was so deep within her that he had the odd notion they were permanently attached.

She grinned down at him, squeezing delightedly with the muscles in her buttocks. Then she began to rotate her hips very slowly. Longarm lay back and let Stella enjoy herself. She knew precisely what she was doing, prolonging their climax as long as possible, pausing in her hip rotations more and more often, for shorter and shorter periods, as she gradually gave in to her own mounting pleasure.

Abruptly, her long curls streaming down over Longarm's face and shoulders, she began rocking herself back and forth until at last, with a deep groan of joy, she poured her juices down over him in a hot, delicious explosion that sent her falling forward upon his chest, limp and trembling.

Longarm had been holding himself back, intent only on her pleasure. Now he rolled her over and thrust deep within, his knees astride her hips.

"Oh, my God, Custis!" she cried. "Again? So soon! I don't know if I can!"

"Sure you can. Just lie back and let it happen, Stella."

He was already thrusting with full, slow, even strokes. Determined not to hurry, he used only part of his weight and strength. He had told her to lie back and relax and, still panting from her own wild ride a moment before, that was what she did at first.

But gradually she came to life under him. Longarm felt her exhausted inner muscles reviving, responding to his measured, metronomic thrusts. She began to meet his thrusts, to move faster, to drive up at him still harder. Tiny cries of astonished delight broke from her. She kept her eyes shut tightly and began to snap her head back and forth.

Longarm was on his own now, building to the final explosion. It had been a long time coming for both of them, but by this time their bodies had taken over, and with mounting fierceness they slammed at each other recklessly as short grunts broke from her lips. Her body was now pulsing wildly under him, keeping time with him. With a sudden fierce cry, she flung both arms up around his neck and arched her body up at him. Longarm pounded in hard to meet her thrust—and then he was over the edge himself, pulsing out of control, emptying, his shaft throbbing almost painfully, until at last he was drained, this time completely.

Utterly spent, he rolled off her and rested his soaking face in the sweet nest of her auburn curls.

When their breathing had quieted, Stella said softly, her fingers tracing the outline of his ear, "That was nice, Custis. So very nice. You have no idea how long I've waited for something like this to happen to me . . . again."

He rested his lips against one of her trembling eyelids. Then, with his lips, he brushed her forehead. "I'm glad, Stella."

"Are you still going to leave? Won't you stay another night?"

"You know I'd like that, Stella. But I have business in Dun Creek—business that has been delayed considerable because of my injury."

"There's nothing I can say to make you stay a while longer?"

"Nothing," he said gently.

"I could use that poker in the kitchen and bang your head some more. It doesn't seem to affect you permanently, but you'd sure have to stay a while longer, then."

"Please don't. Just the thought of it makes me wince."

She laughed and got up from the bed and began to dress. "I'll tell Abe to saddle your black. The ride to Dun Creek will take only a few hours. You should get there before dark."

As Stella finished dressing and went out to find Abe, Longarm sat up and reached for his longjohns. Stella had made a joke of it, but she was not pleased he was going. Still, there was no way Longarm was going to involve her in this case. He had come to Dun Creek to track down the Mullin Gang, and that was about all he could handle for now.

Of course, if he should happen to meet up with Pete Davis again, he'd be most grateful. But that kind of luck seemed highly unlikely. Davis would be long out of this territory by now.

With these somber thoughts occupying him, he stood up and pulled on his pants. By the time he was fully dressed once more, Stella was standing in the bedroom doorway, her hair still reaching down past her shoulders.

"Abe's brought your horse around."

"Thank you, Stella."

He walked over to her and, standing in the doorway, pulled her close to him. "I'll be back. That's a promise. When I get this business taken care of. Okay?"

"Sure," she said. "You'll always be welcome."

He smiled. "Thanks. I appreciate that."

She kissed him full on the lips, then leaned away and reached back for something she had been keeping on a small table by the kitchen doorway. It was a brown Stetson in perfect condition.

71

"It was my first husband's," she told him, handing it to him. "I'm sure he'd want you to have it."

Grinning, Longarm pressed it gently down onto his bandaged head. It fit rather tightly. With the bandages off, he knew, it would be a perfect fit.

"Thank you, Stella," he said. "Soon's I get to Dun Creek, I'll hunt up that doc that never got here and have him see to these bandages."

"I suggest you wait until he's sober," she advised.

"I will."

He kissed her again, reveling in the warmth of her lips, the clean smell of her. Then he pulled himself away and strode toward the door. She followed him out of the ranch house and watched as he mounted. Abe was standing by the black.

"Thanks for the haircut, Abe," Longarm said.

Abe just grinned.

Both of them were still standing before the ranch house when he turned one last time to wave goodbye.

Chapter 5

It was a little past sunset when Longarm rode into Dun Creek. Across from the town's single hotel, he saw a sign, STILES LIVERY, and made for it. The few punchers and townspeople passing on the boardwalks tried not to stare at his bandaged head or the curious way his hat sat atop it. Longarm paid scant attention as he dismounted in front of the livery stable and led his horse inside the barn.

He was lifting off his bedroll when a tall, stooped man in his late thirties with a light thatch of red hair covering his freckled head approached him. He sniffed and snorted nervously, resembling the horses he was currying. In fact, his face did seem a mite longer than the average.

"Go light on the oats," Longarm said, "and give him a good rubdown."

"That'll make it two bits, mister."

Longarm flipped a coin at him. The fellow's long hand snatched the piece out of the air with the quickness of a striking rattlesnake.

"Are you Stiles, the owner of this place?"

"Nope. Stiles is the thief what sold me this stable ten years ago." The man sent a black dart of tobacco juice at a spill of hay on the floor. "Ain't got around to changing the sign yet. People call me Hoss."

"Where can I find Doc Gilmore?"

"Try his office, back of the barbershop. Or Steadman's saloon. More than likely he'll be in the saloon, getting a good start on the night ahead of him."

Longarm nodded, left the livery carrying his gear, and crossed the street to the hotel. He registered, stashed his gear in his room on the second floor, then left the hotel and proceeded down the walk to Steadman's saloon. The place was noisy, the air layered with coiling blue smoke, the sawdust on the floor no longer clean. The stench of tobacco smoke, unwashed bodies, and sweaty feet filled the place.

Stopping at the bar, he asked the barkeep if Doc Gilmore was around. Wordlessly, the barkeep tipped his head, indicating a table at the back. Longarm saw a paunchy fellow in a dirty frock coat and battered bowler hat slumped over a whiskey. He was not yet down for the count, but he looked close.

Longarm strode over to his table, picked up a nearby chair, and placed it down alongside the doctor's table.

Then he straddled the seat and rested his arms on the back of the chair.

"Doc?"

The doctor glanced at him. His eyes were bloodshot but surprisingly alert. "Yes?" he said clearly.

"I'd like you to take a look at my head."

He glanced up at the bandages, the ghost of a smile on his seamed face. "Have to take the bandages off first."

"I'll pay."

"Cash?"

Longarm nodded.

"My boy, you have just found a physician."

He got up with surprising alacrity and preceded Longarm out through the saloon. Longarm caught up to him on the boardwalk.

"My offices are behind the barbershop," Doc Gilmore told him. "Enlighten me, sir. What is the nature of your injuries?"

"I was clubbed about the head with a gun barrel."

"Fine," he said enthusiastically. "I was afraid it might be a very bad case of head lice."

Inside his office, the doctor lit a lamp on his desk, then groped his way into a larger room. Longarm followed after him and stood by while he lit a second lamp. This room contained an army cot and a small stool before a wall cabinet containing medical supplies. A microscope gathered dust on a small work table and in one corner a pale skeleton dangled.

"Sit down on the stool," the doctor told him.

Longarm did as he was told. Before the doctor

started to unwind the bandages, he took a whiskey bottle from the wall cabinet, poured himself a shot, and downed it. With surprising gentleness, he then proceeded to unravel the bandage.

Not until he got down to the clipped skull did it become particularly painful. He was exceedingly careful as he lifted off this final layer of bandages. Only in a few places did the bandage take scab tissue with it. Emptying whiskey from his bottle onto a clean bandage, the doctor swabbed gently at the lacerations until he had thoroughly cleaned Longarm's nearly barren skull.

"You've had a fine nurse, mister," Gilmore said. "Your scalp is as pink as a baby's ass and there's no sign of infection. You've got some pretty mean scars there, but your hair should grow out soon and cover it all. Who was the nurse?"

"Stella Loman."

"That would be Bob Loman's wife."

"Yes."

"Poor woman. She deserves a better man than that."

"Yes."

"That'll be two dollars."

Longarm counted out the coins and handed the doctor his fee. "I won't have to keep any more bandages on it?"

"Perhaps not a bandage. But certainly a clean handkerchief or a fresh cloth of some kind should be kept between the hatband and your skull. And I suggest you make sure you keep the skull clean until all the scars have closed over completely. There's still a slim chance of infection if you reopen any of those lacerations. Might be a good idea to wash your head off with whiskey every once in a while."

"I'll remember that."

"Thank you, sir. Your payment was prompt, as you promised."

The doctor turned off his lamps and followed Longarm out of his office. After the doctor had locked up, the two stood in the darkening street as the desultory night traffic flowed past the barbershop.

"Doc . . . ?"

"Yes?"

"About a week ago, did an old codger from Bromfield arrive in town with a coffin—a coffin containing the remains of Connie Hardin?"

"Hardin's daughter? Why, yes, he did."

"You got any idea where that old reprobate is now? I was wondering if he went back to Bromfield yet."

"As a matter of fact, I heard Hardin gave him a job on his spread as a wrangler." The doctor turned to look at him. "You know about that business, do you?"

"Some of it."

"Then you know how badly poor Hardin took it. First his wife, then his daughter. She was a wild one, but he loved her. Hell, we all did—those of us who saw her grow up."

"What's the best way for me to get out to Hardin's spread?"

"The Lazy H is due north of here. Take the mill road out of town and follow it till the river branches.

Continue along the left fork, heading for a mountain pass you'll see dead ahead. You can't miss it."

"How far is it?"

"A good three-hour ride."

"Thanks."

"Join me in a drink?" the doctor asked.

"Nope. Figure I'll get me some shuteye."

"Then I'll bid you good night, sir."

"Good night, " Longarm replied.

Longarm left the doctor, crossed the street, and entered the hotel. This was his first day up and about and he was all of a sudden mighty weary. That bit of bed calisthenics before he left the Bar S hadn't helped either—not that he regretted it.

As he drifted off to sleep a little later, the last thing on his mind was the ride he planned to make to the Lazy H first thing in the morning. He was anxious to get it over with. It would not be pleasant to talk to a man who had just lost his only daughter, and Longarm was prepared to lie some—a strategem he did not much relish. Yet he didn't see that he had much choice. The bereaved father needed to have some kind of explanation, and it was important that he be left with something that would give him comfort. And that Longarm was determined to do.

When he awoke the next morning, the heavy fatigue that had clubbed him into a dreamless sleep had vanished with the new day. He attended to his toilet, dressed quickly, and was on his black riding out of Dun Creek before eight o'clock. By mid-morning he found himself on Lazy H range, judging from the

"Howdy, stranger," the man called, stepping out onto the porch. "Light and set a spell."

"Much obliged," said Longarm, dismounting.

"Name's Clem Hardin," the cattleman said, as Longarm joined him on the porch. His powerful voice was surprisingly soft.

"I'm Custis Long," Longarm told him.

The two men shook hands.

"We can sit over here," Hardin said, indicating a wicker table and some chairs a few feet away.

As soon as they were settled, an old Indian woman pattered out onto the porch carrying a tray with coffee, sugar, and cream—and two large mugs. While she poured the coffee for them, Longarm studied Hardin. He had a solid, craggy face that radiated strength, not only of purpose, but of design as well. Yet Longarm had the sense when he looked into his eyes that Hardin had been struck a terrible, nearly fatal blow; that, deep beneath the solidity of his countenance, something vital had cracked and would never be whole again.

After pouring out their coffee, the Indian woman left them. Reluctant to bring up at once his purpose in coming to the Lazy H, Longarm commented on the neatness and apparent prosperity of the ranch. Hardin responded politely, patiently, making no effort to pry from Longarm the purpose of his visit. But at last a silence yawned between them, and Longarm knew he could delay mention of Connie no longer.

"I knew Connie," he said, placing his empty cup down.

Hardin nodded. "I expected as much when I saw

you ride in. Randy said someone had paid him to see that her coffin got here safely. But he was sure that you had been killed by the same man who killed Connie."

"Nearly killed," Longarm said.

"Would you care to explain?"

"That's why I rode out, Mr. Hardin."

"Call me Clem. You were my daughter's friend, I gather."

"I met her on the train," Longarm lied smoothly. "She talked a lot about you and this spread. She was pleased to be coming back home, as she put it. She had grown to hate Denver's noise and crowds. Her husband was a teamster, and on the road a lot. She had decided to leave him and she wanted to start over again, here in this valley. Her last words were of you. She requested that she be buried on the knoll near her mother. She said you would know the site, that you and she had talked of it once."

"Yes," he said. "We had."

Hardin looked down at his coffee. His face had turned to stone. Longarm had the impression that, if he struck it, pieces of flint would flake off. Then Hardin cleared his throat and looked again at Longarm.

"Her husband...did she mention him in any detail?"

"Only that he was not very kind to her. She told me she was fleeing from a madman. He just didn't take kindly to the notion of her leaving him. I told her to be careful. From what she told me of him, I knew he was about as peaceable as a grizzly. I feel partly responsible for her death. I shouldn't have left her alone in that hotel."

"There is no reason for you to blame yourself. From what Randy Walls told me, Connie was right. She was fleeing a madman. He stormed up the hotel stairs and burst into her room like a man possessed. Had you been with her, you might have been killed your self. Indeed, as I mentioned before, didn't he almost kill you later?"

Longarm nodded and related briefly to Hardin his attempt to trap Davis and how it had backfired.

"Why do you suppose he was so anxious to kill you, as well?"

Longarm thought fast. "He must've seen us on the train and later entering the same hotel. He was sure a jealous man."

"Can you describe him to me?"

Longarm described Pete Davis to Hardin. By the time Longarm had finished, Hardin's face had gone ashen. "I have seen that man."

"When?"

"On the same day I rode in to pick up Connie's . . . coffin."

"Where?"

"I was in Steadman's saloon. I had not yet gone to the funeral parlor. I guess I was a little shaky. At that moment I needed the courage you get from whiskey. I didn't want to embarrass the friends who had ridden down with me."

"You don't have to explain," Longarm said gently.

"As I left the saloon to go across to the funeral parlor, this man you have just described brushed past me on his way into the saloon. From his brusque and impatient manner, I had no alternative but to notice him. What you said about his eyes, his dark, complexion, his size—it all fits."

"Do you know where this man is now?"

"No. I didn't see him again that day, and I have not seen him since."

Longarm leaned back in his chair, frowning in thought. There was a chance Pete Davis was still around, but it was not too likely. He must have followed Randy on in to Dun Creek and then hung around for a while to make sure he had finished Longarm off that night.

"Before you leave, Mr. Long, I would like to reimburse you for your expenses."

"Forget it."

"I insist. The coffin, the rental of that spring wagon, and the amount you paid Randy to drive the wagon must have amounted to a not inconsiderable sum. And Connie was my daughter, sir."

Longarm shrugged. "All right. As you wish. By the way, I'd like to speak to Randy. I figure he'd appreciate an explanation. Last he knew, I was crow bait. He seemed a mite shocked when I rode in."

Hardin smiled thinly and got to his feet. "By all means. And it would give me great pleasure if you would join me for the noon meal."

"That's kind of you. I'd be delighted."

With a brisk nod, Hardin left Longarm and went

inside. Longarm descended the porch steps and started for the horse barn. Before he reached it, he heard Randy calling to him from the bunkhouse. Pulling up, Longarm turned to see Randy standing in the bunkhouse doorway, holding Longarm's Winchester in his hand.

"I was just keepin' it for you," Randy said, as Longarm walked toward him.

Three curious ranch hands had joined Randy in front of the bunkhouse by this time, but they kept discreetly back as Longarm pulled up in front of Randy. Smiling his thanks, Longarm took the rifle from Randy. Then he reached out and shook the old man's hand heartily.

"Hell, man," said Longarm, "you ought to keep this. You saved my life. Davis would have finished me off for sure if you hadn't gone after him when you did."

"Didn't look like I'd saved your life at the time."

"I couldn't talk or move. But I could see you clear enough, and I heard every word you said. I guess I was pretty well smashed up, but the next morning I was able to crawl to my horse. I gave him his head and he got me to a ranch house not too far away."

Randy grinned. "That head of yours must be made of cast iron."

Longarm took off his hat, removed the handkerchief, and showed Randy his scalped locks and the road map of scars that were still not fully healed. Randy whistled softly.

The two talked quietly for a while longer. Randy

was pleased to be working on a ranch once again, and he seemed to like working for Clem Hardin. He swore to Longarm he would never go back to working as a bellhop, even if every hotel patron tipped as liberally as Longarm did.

Laughing softly at that crack, Longarm thanked Randy again, nodded to the other ranch hands, and walked back to the ranch house with his Winchester. He was not looking forward to joining Connie's father in his noon meal, even though Hardin was holding himself together well enough. It was damned painful to see what the effort was taking out of the man.

An hour or so later, at the conclusion of the quiet, somber meal, Longarm waited a decent interval, then made his excuses. The rancher walked with Longarm out onto the porch. As the two men shook hands, Hardin's face became suddenly iron with resolve.

"Long," he said, "if you ever come upon this fellow Pete Davis, I would appreciate it if you would give me a crack at him."

"You sure you mean that?"

"I never meant anything more."

Longarm considered a moment. Since there seemed very little chance of any such eventuality, he said, "All right, sir. I'll remember."

"Thank you. And thank you again for coming."

A moment later, moving out through the gate astride his black, Longarm glanced back at the ranch house and saw the white-haired father of Connie Hardin Davis still standing on the porch watching him ride out.

Longarm waved his hand in farewell, then turned his thoughts to what lay ahead. He had been sent up here to track down the informant willing to help the government nail the Mullin gang. So far, he had made damned little progress in that direction. It was about time he got cracking. As he saw it, his first order of business was to contact that informant, something he had better tend to as soon as he returned to Dun Creek.

He lifted his horse to a canter.

Chapter 6

In the alley behind Steadman's saloon, Bob Loman felt something moist nudging his cheek. He stirred fitfully, then opened his eyes to see a mangy, lop-eared dog sniffing hopefully at him.

"Damn you! Get away!" Loman cried hoarsely, his hand groping for something to throw at the animal.

Jumping back, the dog ran off down the alley, its tail between its legs.

Loman shook his head to clear it of the hammering ache and became aware at once that he needed a hair of the dog that bit him. His stomach was an aching void and his limbs trembled like an old man's. Reaching out shakily, he grabbed the side of the outhouse and managed to pull himself upright. The stale odor of vomit and another, viler stench seemed to cling to him like a curse. He looked down at his damp crotch and realized he had soiled himself during the night. He moistened his dry lips and tried to recall the events of the night before.

Gradually the shards of memory came together. He saw himself lurching through the back door and into the back alley, the hooting laughter of those who had demeaned and robbed him following out after him. He had been heading for this privy, but he had been unable to guide his steps properly and had crashed into the side of it. He remembered dimly trying to get up, then collapsing into his own vomit, evacuating his bowels and bladder at the same time.

Desolation filled him. When this day ended, he would not be on his way to California. The stage would leave without him. All the money Paxman had given him was gone, every cent of it. He had been robbed by those card sharks, including the sheriff. They had plied him with drinks, insuring that he would be unable to detect their crooked play. When he had understood at last what they were about and protested, they had punched him about brutally, then sent him reeling into the alley.

Remembering that part of it, Loman moved his shoulders and arms and felt the bruised spots, the fresh, sharp aches. Reaching up to his face, he found that his lips were swollen. When he closed his eyes, he felt the flesh about his right eye pull painfully. It was almost swollen shut, he realized.

What to do? He could not go back to Mullin. Mullin had told him, with those sightless eyes trained horribly on him, that if he did not leave on this day's stage, Mullin would see him dead within twenty-four hours. Mullin wanted him out of the territory, and California, he figured, was just far enough.

Loman gathered himself together, then lurched toward the back door to the saloon. Maybe he could get a drink from Big Jim Steadman. He pushed through the door and entered the saloon. It was still early. The swamper had just finished mopping the floor and was throwing fresh sawdust down onto it. The chairs were upside down on the tables. Big Jim was busy behind the bar.

Loman made it to the bar and hung on to it hopefully. Big Jim turned and saw him.

"Jesus Christ, are you back already?"

"I need a drink, Jim."

"You need a whole hell of a lot more than that," Steadman told him.

"Please, Jim. Just a snifter—something to get me going."

Swearing in disgust, Big Jim slapped a shotglass down on the mahogany, then filled it with his cheapest rotgut.

His hands trembling with eagerness, Loman reached out for the drink and, with infinite care, brought the shotglass up to his lips. With one quick dip of his head, he threw the whiskey down his gullet. Then he put down the empty glass, feeling better already, and looked with hope at Big Jim.

"No more, damn you!" Big Jim cried. "Now get the hell out of here. You stink worse'n a dead Indian. And *stay* out!"

Big Jim's words were like slaps. Loman pushed himself away from the bar, turned, and lurched out through the batwings. Hanging on to the porch post, he spied Stiles Livery across the street and remembered the horse he had left there the day before. He had not thought he would ever need it again, but he needed it now. He plunged across the street.

A thought occurred to him. Perhaps Hoss would let him use his tub to clean up, and maybe stake him to some grub. Then Bob Loman would ride out of this town, leave it in the dust, and never come back.

Never!

Reaching Dun Creek that same afternoon, Longarm dismounted in front of the express office and went inside. There he wrote a brief note, folded it, then requested the clerk to place it in Post Office Box 21. This accomplished, Longarm crossed the street to Stiles Livery, left his horse, then went next door to Ma's Restaurant, where he had breakfasted that morning.

He selected a corner table by the window. Just as he sat down, he glimpsed Bob Loman plunging erratically across the street, narrowly missing a dray cart and a sulky. As Longarm understood it, Loman would soon be taking the stage south on his way to California. But, watching Loman disappear in the direction of the livery stable, Longarm wondered if the man would make it. Bob Loman did not seem capable of finishing anything he started.

Some time later, Longarm was sipping his third cup of coffee and beginning to get restless. In his note to the informant he had left in Box 21, he had written that if he still wanted to make a deal with the government, a deputy U. S. marshal would be waiting in Ma's Restaurant for the next four days between three and four thirty each afternoon.

Careful not to disturb his derringer watch fob, Longarm took out his watch and saw that he had half an hour yet to go. He slipped the watch back into his vest pocket and sipped his coffee carefully. He had to make this cup last. Any more coffee and he would never sleep again.

Two other parties had entered the restaurant during his wait: a settler, his wife, and their two boys, both possessing remarkably high, piping voices; and a quiet, intent group of four punchers in their early twenties. From the brief snatches of conversation Longarm caught occasionally, the cowpokes appeared to be on their way back to Texas.

Glancing restlessly out the window, Longarm saw Stella.

She was on a second-story landing, leaving the office of a Land Office lawyer. Longarm remembered then that she had told him she had business in Dun Creek. Recalling what the foreman of the Diamond T had told her the day before, Longarm had a pretty good idea what Stella and that lawyer of hers had been discussing. He wondered what the lawyer might have told her.

He watched her descend the outside stairs to the sidewalk, then move off down the street. For a moment he wanted to leave the restaurant and intercept her, perhaps ask her to join him at dinner in the hotel later that evening. But he had already told himself that it would be best if he did not see her again. And he was certain that, despite what they had told each other the day before, she understood as he did that they could never really hope for anything more than what they had already known.

Stella vanished from his sight and he sat back in his chair, suddenly restless. It occurred to him that he might spend the next four afternoons sitting in this restaurant drinking coffee, all to no avail. What assurance had he that the informant was still living in this town or even near it? The letter had been sent to Washington some time ago, and there was a good chance that whoever had sent it had long since cleared out, along with the Mullin Gang.

The possibility that the letter had been written by a woman no longer bothered Longarm. More than likely, the gang member willing to cooperate simply couldn't write and had been forced to dictate the letter to his girl friend or his wife.

The waitress appeared at his table, a steaming coffee pot in her hand. He quickly placed his hand over his half-empty cup.

"No more for now," he said.

"Will you be wanting to order soon?"

"Maybe."

"We begin serving supper at four-thirty."

"I'll keep that in mind."

The waitress left, obviously unhappy that she had not at least been able to refill his cup.

He glanced again at his watch, then looked up. He was startled to see Stella standing over him.

"Custis! What are you doing here?"

Longarm stared up at her, momentarily flustered. Recovering quickly, he got to his feet. "I just stopped in for a cup of coffee," he told her. "Join me."

She glanced around her, as if she were looking for someone, then looked back at him. Smiling quickly, she said, "All right."

She sat down, Longarm adjusting the chair for her. She thanked him and he sat back down.

"This is quite a surprise," she said.

"Yes. For me, too. I saw you leave the lawyer's office. What did he tell you?"

"He said not to worry. He was sure a judge or a court of law would stand by me if it came to any dispute concerning Bar S business. The fact that I was married to Bob for such a short time would help too, he said."

"Then you've got nothing to worry about."

"Not exactly. I have a partner I did not want, and I will have to deal with this difficulty for some time, I'm afraid."

Longarm leaned back in his chair and waved to the

waitress, indicating more coffee. He had about decided that his informer was not going to show up, so he might as well just relax and enjoy Stella's company. She seemed nervous, however, and was still glancing about her often. For a long moment she peered closely at the four Texans. Then at last she looked back at Longarm, a tiny frown creasing her forehead.

"Custis, have you been here long?" she asked.

"Since three."

"Has there been anyone else in here during that time?"

"No, there hasn't."

She sighed nervously, looked around her once more, then back at Longarm. "What time is it now?"

He consulted his watch. "A quarter after four."

"You were looking at your watch when I came in."

He smiled. "As a matter of fact, yes."

She moistened her lips and leaned closer. In a soft, barely audible whisper, she asked, "Custis, are you waiting to meet someone here?"

In that instant Longarm knew who she was. "Stella!" he said with sudden urgency, his voice low. "Are *you* the one who wrote that letter to Washington?"

She reached into her purse, took out the note Longarm had just left in Post Office Box 21, and pushed it across the table to him. "Did you write this?"

Longarm nodded, then took the letter Vail had given him out of his wallet. A tight smile on his face, he handed it to her. "Is this your handwriting?"

She glanced at it quickly. "Yes."

"Then you're the informant."

"And *you're* the deputy U. S. marshal."

With his hand, Longarm indicated that Stella should keep her voice low. Then he leaned close. "My God, Stella, why did you write that letter?"

"It's a long story."

"Make it as brief as you can."

"We can't talk here," she said.

"You're right. I have a room at the hotel. Let's go there."

"But people will see us."

"Then I'll go first. You follow after me. It's room number twelve, on the second floor in front."

She nodded.

Longarm left some coins on the table, took his leave of Stella, then left the restaurant and crossed the street to his hotel. He was in his room about five minutes before Stella tapped lightly on his door. He pulled it open and she hurried inside.

Sitting beside him on the bed, she told him why she had written that letter to Washington. When she first met Bob, he had worked for Paxman. He seemed quite nice, a cowhand who knew his business. After she married him, however, all that changed radically, and in his fits of drunkenness he began boasting of his past—particularly of his past as a member of the Mullin Gang.

At first she had found it difficult to believe, but the more he told her, the more uncertain she became. At last she began to question him when he was drunk, even pretending to be drunk herself, and it was not long before she was convinced that he had been telling

97

her the truth after all. Not only had he been a member of the Mullin gang, but Jim Paxman himself was really Jim Mullin, holing up at the Diamond T, waiting for a chance to pull his next job. Had it not been for Mullin's blindness, Loman told Stella, there would have been quite a few spectacular raises in this territory, more than enough to eclipse the Daltons or the James gang.

"And when you became convinced Bob was telling you the truth," Longarm suggested, "you wrote the letter."

"Not right away. First I told Bob I would leave him if he did not quit the gang. He said he couldn't. Then, one night, he admitted he might leave the gang if the government would give him a break."

"And that was when you suggested he turn informer."

"Yes. I had heard of such things before. I knew that at best he might get a year, but that would be all, and the world would be rid of the Mullin Gang."

"And Bob agreed to it?"

"He did that night, yes. But he was drunk and pleading with me, and I had been..." She sighed. "...I had been keeping him from my bed. He wanted me desperately. So he agreed to turn informer. I wrote the letter that night and posted it the next day without telling him."

"And when you brought the matter up later..."

"Yes," she said, sighing. "He told me he had been drunk, that he had said what he had only to get me into bed."

"And under no circumstances would he turn informer."

She nodded. "So, of course, I didn't dare tell him I sent the letter. He's terrified, Custis. And ... well, I don't blame him."

"And now he's on his way to California."

"Yes."

"Well, this much, at least, we have accomplished. We now know where the Mullin Gang has been holing up all this time."

"But can't you go out and arrest them now?"

"On whose testimony?"

"Mine, and on what Bob told me."

"No. It's not nearly enough. You can't testify against your husband, don't forget. And there is one thing about the Mullin Gang that makes it very difficult for the Pinkertons and the rest of us."

"What's that?"

"Each member of the gang was always very careful to keep his face well covered during a job. As a result, no eyewitness could ever be found to give us a physical description of any of the men."

"So there would be no one to back up my testimony."

Longarm nodded. "And I am sure that if it came to a trial, half the population of this territory would swear that Paxman and his ranch hands were all peace-loving, law-abiding citizens, who could not possibly be guilty of such an outrageous charge. And can you imagine the sympathy a blind Jim Mullin would get, testifying to his innocence?"

"Then what can you do?" she asked.

"For now, nothing. We'll just have to keep an eye on them. Sooner or later, they'll bust loose. Maybe they won't rob a bank or hold up a train, but they'll do something. And then we'll be waiting."

She nodded. "Bob said that Mullin was planning a raise, as he called it. He said that, even though Mullin was blind, he was planning to go along."

Longarm shook his head in wonderment. "It's in his blood, robbing trains and banks. He can't get along without it."

With a weary sigh, Stella got to her feet. "I must get back," she said.

"You won't stay for dinner?" he asked, as he stood up also.

She shook her head. "It's been a very confusing— and wearying—day for me, Custis. I just want to get back to the Bar S and sit down and see which way I should go next. After what my lawyer told me, I'm not sure if I shouldn't just sell out to Paxman—or Mullin. As it is now, I have as a partner the leader of a famous band of outlaws."

He bent and kissed her lightly on the forehead. She placed her hand behind his head and pressed his face down to hers again. This time they kissed full on the lips.

"There!" she said. "That's better. Now, what are your plans?"

"I'm going to have to wire my chief in Denver and find out. Until I hear otherwise, surveillance is all I can manage."

"Bob is taking the stage out tonight."

"I know."

"My place would be a fine spot from which to watch Mullin."

"We'll see."

"Is there any chance, Custis, that anyone else here in Dun Creek knows who you are?"

"I don't see how—if you don't tell, I won't "

"But, Custis, who was it that beat you so fearfully before you reached my place? Was it one of the Diamond T hands?"

He smiled ruefully. "No, Stella. That was some business left over from Denver. I'd prefer not to talk about it now."

"Oh, I see. All right, then."

She went to the door. He opened it for her and let her out. Then he went to the window and watched for her. When she left the hotel a few minutes later, he kept his eye on her until she vanished down the street, heading in the direction of the lawyer's office. Longarm assumed she had left her spring wagon in front of it.

A moment later he saw her driving the wagon on her way out of town, and left the window. Slumping down on the bed, he began to compose mentally the telegram he would be sending off to Billy Vail the next day.

Hoss had not been kind. In exchange for clean clothes and enough money for a decent stake, he had made Loman work. All that afternoon, Loman had been kept busy cleaning out stalls and feeding and watering and currying the horses.

But Loman's torment ended a little after four that afternoon, after which, fully dressed, cold sober at last, with a decent amount of cash in his pockets, he prepared to leave the stable and ride out. Behind Loman in the livery's small office, crumpled behind a makeshift desk, Hoss lay dead, the manure-smeared tines of a pitchfork thrust through his heart and lungs.

Loman was approaching the stable door, leading his horse, when he saw Custis Long leave Ma's Restaurant and cross the street to the hotel. Loman pulled back into the livery's entrance to watch and a few minutes later saw Stella follow Long from the restaurant. Fuming, Loman watched his wife disappear into the hotel.

There was no doubt in Loman's mind what was going on. Stella was going to Long's room. She hadn't been able to get enough of him while he was living under their roof. And now, like a bitch in heat, she was chasing him all the way into Dun Creek.

Her own husband she had banished from her bed. But for this man she would open her legs anywhere, any time. . . .

Trembling with rage, Loman mounted up and rode out of town. He had intended to head south, but his fury would not let him. After killing Hoss, it was dangerous for him to stay close by. But he was not going to let that bitch escape unscathed. She had humiliated him . . . scorned him. If he was on the run now, an outcast, a murderer, it was all her fault.

He headed for the Bar S. There he would wait for Stella to finish with her lover and return home. It would be his turn then. And this time, damn it, he would not take no for an answer.

He would take what was his, whether she liked it or not.

Chapter 7

Longarm was in the hotel bar, drinking what passed
for Maryland rye, when he heard the commotion outside. Sticking his cheroot in his mouth, he left his
table and walked out onto the porch to see what was
going on. As he pulled up to one side of the hotel
door, he saw the sheriff and the town constable hurrying from Steadman's saloon. They were heading
across the street to Stiles Livery.

Through the smoke of his cheroot, Longarm
watched as the sheriff and the constable plunged into
the livery stable. By that time the word had reached
the crowd on the street and those townsmen on the
hotel porch.

Hoss had just been found murdered in his office. Someone had driven a pitchfork through his heart.

As the crowd outside the livery swelled, Longarm pushed his way down the hotel steps, then moved across the street and through the growing ranks of spectators. A few tried to resist his passage, but one look up at Longarm's grim, intent face and they stepped aside. Once inside the stable, Longarm followed the sound of an angry burst of conversation and came to the doorway of a cramped office. Keeping just outside the door, he looked into it.

Doc Gilmore was in the act of dropping a horse blanket over the dead man while the sheriff and the town constable stood on the other side of the desk, arguing.

"... and I say it was Bob Loman!" the constable insisted. "Hoss made him clean out the stables before giving him a change of clothes or any money. He was working Loman's ass off, and I could see how Loman was taking it when I came in for my horse."

"That don't mean a thing," insisted the sheriff. "Bob Loman is a lush and a lousy gambler, but he sure as hell wouldn't've done this to Hoss. Hell, he and Hoss were drinkin' buddies."

"Not lately they weren't."

"I think you're crazy."

"If you don't swear out a warrant for Bob Loman, sheriff, I'll..."

"You'll do what, Skinner? Who got you this job, anyway? You'll eat my shit if I say so. Now, get out

106

of here with your fool notions. It was a robbery, plain and simple. Some drifter killed Hoss!"

Longarm stepped into the office at that moment. "There were four Texans in Ma's Restaurant this afternoon," he offered. "Maybe one of them did it."

The sheriff spun about to face Longarm. Longarm saw what amounted to a flickering, momentary recognition of himself—as if the sheriff knew who Longarm was. But it lasted only an instant. The sheriff's beefy face went suddenly red. He was a man in his late forties, still powerful about the shoulders but getting uncomfortably heavy about the middle. His face had the texture of old leather. His eyes were narrow blue slits that did not waver as they met Longarm's steady gaze. A dusty star was pinned to the man's vest.

"Who the hell are you, mister?" the sheriff demanded.

Without replying directly, Longarm went on, "And, then again, there was a settler in the restaurant with his wife and two kids. Them two boys seemed mighty rambunctious. Maybe you ought to check them out, too."

Longarm's sarcasm was not lost on the sheriff. His eyes narrowed meanly. "You goin' to tell me who you are, mister—and what right you got to come bustin' in here like this?"

"He's a citizen," said Doc Gilmore, standing up and straightening his shoulders wearily. "His name is Custis Long." The doctor smiled at Longarm as he

107

retreated from behind the desk. "How's your head?"

"Fine, Doc."

"This here is Sheriff Gulch," the doctor said. "This is a miserable crime, but he has already absolved the most likely suspect. I agree with the constable. Bob Loman did it. He had the opportunity and the motive."

"The motive?"

"The sheriff and his buddies cleaned him out last night. Loman awoke today with not a penny to his name. I am sure he left this stable considerably richer than when he walked in to plead with Hoss for help."

"Damn it, Doc!" cried the sheriff. "You don't know what in hell you're talking about!"

The doctor looked at the sheriff for a long moment, then shook his head wearily and pushed past him and out of the office. "The undertaker's waiting," he said, "and I'm thirsty."

The sheriff swung around to Longarm. "Get out of here, Long. This ain't none of your affair." His eyes narrowed craftily. "Or is it?"

"I just came for my horse," Longarm drawled. He turned and left the small office.

A moment later, his black saddled, his Winchester in the rifle scabbard, Longarm led his horse out of the stable and through the growing crowd. Mounting up, he rode out of town. Not until he was out of sight of Dun Creek's buildings did he turn his mount loose.

Then he lifted his black to a gallop. A terrible sense of foreboding concerning Stella and Bob Loman had fallen over him. If Loman had been working in that stable all afternoon, he could easily have seen Stella follow Longarm into the hotel. A man who would kill as Bob Loman just had would not sit still for what he had seen. What little control Bob Loman had been able to exercise over himself until now had evidently collapsed completely.

Loman had become that most dangerous of all wild beasts: a desperate, deranged killer.

Stella entered the kitchen wearily, moved through it to the small sitting room, and dropped her handbag onto the top of the rolltop desk. Opening the bag, she took out the written agreement concerning the Bar S she had signed with Bob at the time of their marriage, then took out the Bar S mortgage. She had brought both documents with her into Dun Creek, assuming that she would need them when discussing Bob's sale of his interest in the ranch to Paxman.

Glancing only cursorily now at both documents, she shoved them into their accustomed pigeonhole, then took out the letter she had mailed to Washington, which Deputy U. S. Marshal Custis Long had shown her that afternoon at the restaurant.

She read it through once again, shuddered at its potential for trouble, then crumpled it up.

"What's that you got there?"

Horrified, Stella spun around. Bob was standing in the doorway glowering at her. Without thinking, she thrust the hand containing the letter behind her. Bob's eyes narrowed angrily and he strode swiftly into the room. She tried to duck away, but he caught her arm with cruel fingers and flung her against the wall.

"Let's see what you got there! Is it a letter from your lover boy?"

"No!" she cried.

"Let me see!"

He reached around behind her and snatched the letter from her hand. A portion of it was ripped away, but Loman paid no heed as he pulled back, opened up the crumpled letter, and began to read it, his lips moving with almost painful deliberation. Terrified, Stella leaned back against the wall, praying that Loman's poor reading ability would keep the truth from him. But it was a forlorn hope at best, and as soon as he had finished reading the letter, he glanced up at her with blazing eyes.

"You sent this?" he demanded.

She did not respond. She just closed her eyes in despair.

He flung the letter to the floor and advanced on her, grabbing her by the shoulders.

"Damn you! You sent it! That's why that deputy marshal is up here. And you told him all about Paxman."

"Yes," she spat, her fury momentarily overcoming her terror. "Yes, I did! And he'll get you! He'll get all of you!"

"No, he won't! Not now!"

He slapped her so hard her head swung around.

Then he slapped her again. She tried to pull free. This time he punched her in the stomach. She knifed forward, and he stepped aside to let her fall onto the floor. She fought for breath, gagging.

Standing over her, Loman smiled. "I'll warn Mullin," he told her. "But first, I'm going to take what's mine. What you've been holdin' out on me!"

"You . . . beast!"

"Yes! And you know what? It feels good! I'm through being kicked around! No one's ever goin' to treat me like you did—never again. I just killed a man today. And Abe's out there in the barn with half his face stove in. I'll kill you next and love every minute of it—if you don't come across!"

Stella looked up at him, saw the red light of madness in his eyes, and realized he was telling the truth.

"Get in there!" he demanded, kicking at her brutally. "Get into that bedroom, or I'll drag you in by the hair!"

Sobbing in terror, Stella stumbled to her feet and headed for the bedroom.

Longarm heard the shots just as he topped the last rise between him and the Bar S. He lifted his black to a gallop and charged around to the rear of the ranch, coming in behind one of the horse barns. Nearing the barn, he snatched his Winchester from its scabbard and leaped from his still moving horse.

As the black pulled up and trotted away, Longarm

ran the remaining distance to the barn and ducked through the rear door. A shot came from the front of the barn, then another. Keeping low, Longarm glided through the barn. Sixgun in hand, Abe was propped up beside a narrow side window, his face a bloody mess. He was firing at the ranch house through the shattered windowpane.

Pulling up beside him, Longarm cranked a fresh cartridge into the Winchester's firing chamber. "Who's in there?" he demanded.

"That son of a bitch Loman," Abe croaked through painfully swollen lips. "I took a shot at him when he tried to walk out. I'm gonna kill him. He's got Stella in there, and she was screamin' something awful."

"Well, if Stella's in there, hold up. You might hit her."

Dazed, Abe looked at Longarm. Then he nodded. "Okay. We'll wait until the bastard tries to come out again."

"You stay here. I'll circle around behind the ranch house."

"I'll cover you."

As Longarm doubled back through the barn, he heard shots—this time coming from the ranch house, with Abe's answering shots coming immediately after.

Cutting through a patch of alders, he made for the rear corner of the ranch house, then flattened himself against the wall. Keeping low, he moved around to the kitchen side. When he reached it, he swore, more loudly this time. One of Abe's stray bullets must have knocked over a lamp. A black plume of smoke was pulsing through a shattered kitchen windowpane. Peering in through the window, Longarm saw great sheets of flame billowing through the dense smoke.

Abruptly, he heard a window shattering from the back of the ranch house. He spun and raced back. Turning the corner, he was just in time to see Bob Loman, who had just flung himself through the bedroom window, scramble to his feet and race toward the alders. Longarm pulled up and fired. His slug struck Loman high in the shoulder and slammed him forward onto the ground. Levering a fresh cartridge into his firing chamber, Longarm started toward Loman.

"Stay down," Longarm commanded, "or I'll blow your head off!"

Instead, Loman rolled quickly over and fired up at him with his Colt. It must have been a double-action. Longarm ducked quickly back as the shower of slugs slammed into the side of the ranch house.

Then came a series of shrieks from inside. It was Stella. Her terrifying screams momentarily transfixed Longarm. From the sound of it, he knew she must be trapped. The wounded Loman scrambled to his feet and vanished through the brush.

Disregarding him, Longarm raced around to the front of the ranch house, charged up to the door, and kicked it in. Pushing his way inside, his forearms over his face, he saw that half the kitchen wall was in flames by this time. He darted past the kitchen door and into the bedroom, pulling up at the foot of the bed.

Naked, Stella was lying on the bedspread, her legs and arms roped to the four corners of the bed. She was no longer screaming, just moaning and coughing feebly as the thick pall of smoke filled the room, drawn by the draft from the shattered window. She had not submitted to her husband easily. Her face was swollen so that her eyes seemed but slits, and her puffed lips were cut and bleeding.

As he bent to untie her feet, she groaned, then opened her eyes. Too distraught or too badly injured to recognize him, she shrieked as he bent over her. Ignoring her cries, he pulled out his knife and cut her loose. Once she was free, she rolled over, still screaming, and hunched herself up on the bed.

Moving as swiftly as he could in the stinging, choking clouds of smoke that pumped into the room, Longarm pulled some dresses and a pair of shoes from the bureau drawer, then wrapped Stella in the dresses, flung her over his shoulder, and ran from the place.

Inside the barn, Longarm put Stella down in the back of her wagon, then looked back at the flaming ranch house. It was a blazing inferno now, with flames breaking through the roof in spots. There was nothing to be done to stop the flames. All he could do was let it burn.

Then he remembered Abe and began calling out to him. But there was no answer. Hurrying back to the side window alongside which Abe had been crouching, Longarm saw a trail of disturbed hay where a heavy body had been dragged across the barn floor and out the rear door. He followed the tracks into the pasture and, some distance from the barn, found Abe's dead body in a narrow ditch, the rope Loman had used to drag him still around his neck.

Longarm hurried back to the barn, found a shovel, and buried Abe as swiftly as he could. Then he went back to Stella. She had regained consciousness, but was curiously listless. He tried to get her to help herself a little, to sit up if she could, but she seemed totally unaware of her surroundings. At last, he dressed her, as he would an uncomplaining invalid. Then he hitched his black up to her wagon and drove into Dun Creek, a silent, listless Stella sitting up beside him on the seat.

It was a little past nine when he pulled up in front of the hotel. As he helped Stella down from her wagon, he collared a youngster and directed him to hurry to Steadman's and bring the doctor to the hotel.

"But...I can't go in *there,* mister! I ain't even supposed to be out this late! My mother, she'll..."

"Pronto, boy!" Longarm snapped. "This is an emergency!"

The boy turned and raced toward the saloon.

Longarm helped Stella into the hotel. The desk clerk frowned slightly when he noted Stella's disheveled appearance and her battered countenance, but Longarm forced himself to ignore this as he obtained his key and started for the steps.

115

Before he reached them, he looked back at the desk clerk. "When Doc Gilmore gets here, send him up to my room."

The clerk nodded.

Just then, the boy Longarm had sent after the doctor burst into the hotel, with Doc Gilmore on his heels.

"Come upstairs with us, Doc," Longarm said. "You got yourself a patient."

When the doctor saw Stella's appearance he seemed shocked, but he held back on any questions as he accompanied them up the stairs. When Longarm finished the climb, he glanced back down the stairs and saw the boy still standing in the small lobby, gaping up at them. Longarm reached into his pocket and threw a quarter down to him. The boy caught it, turned, and scampered from the hotel.

Longarm then helped the still strangely docile Stella to his room. The doctor followed after them. After a quick, expert glance, the doctor asked Longarm to go downstairs and wait in the lobby until he finished a more thorough examination.

Downstairs in the lobby, Longarm sat impatiently in a dusty, faded velvet armchair, fuming. He had a pretty good idea where Bob Loman was heading when he left the Bar S, and that was all the excuse he needed to go after him—and Paxman. If Paxman helped Bob Loman in any way, that would make him an accessory after the fact of murder, and he could go to jail for that, even if he could not for being the leader of the Mullin Gang.

One way or another, Paxman could be made to pay for his crimes.

But first things first. The man Longarm wanted more than any other right now was Bob Loman.

He heard footsteps on the stairs and looked up. The doctor was coming down.

Longarm got up and hurried over to him. "How is she, Doc?"

"Her injuries—physical, that is—are not serious," the doctor said. "What I am worried about is her mental state."

"What do you mean?"

"I'm not sure myself. I suppose it is normal for her to react in this fashion. But it worries me. How long has she been like this?"

"Ever since I took her from the ranch house. On the trip to town, she didn't say a word to me—not a word."

"I could get nothing out of her myself," the doctor replied. "And she seems so . . . so passive, so unresponsive. It is as if she has withdrawn into a shell. Of course, who can blame her, after all she's been through?"

"Is it all right if I go up to see her?"

"Yes, but don't be surprised if you get no response from her. I couldn't get a word out of her. But it *was* her husband that did this, wasn't it?"

Longarm nodded grimly.

"I thought so. He's gone quite mad, it seems. First poor Hoss, now this. He's lost all control." The doctor smiled wanly at Longarm. "I think I need a drink," he said.

Longarm watched him go, then turned and hurried up the stairs to his room. Pushing open the door, he saw Stella sitting on the edge of the bed like a forlorn little girl, staring straight ahead at the wall. Her face was scarlet from the doctor's examination, but aside from that there was no sign she was aware of anything that was going on about her.

Longarm sat down carefully beside her. He put one arm around her shoulder and held her tightly.

"You should cry," he told her, as softly as he could. "It will do you good to cry. Loosen up, Stella."

He looked into her eyes. They seemed not to see him. Longarm had an impulse to pass a hand across her eyes to watch her reaction. Instead, he put his other arm around her shoulder and held her tightly, as close as he could. He felt her awaken and begin to pull away from him.

But he would not let her. He spoke to her, soothingly, softly, until she stopped pushing against his strength and collapsed against him. Her head rested snugly against his shoulder as she buried her face in his chest. She began to shake then, trembling all over, but he kept his arms about her until the shaking and trembling subsided. After that came sobs, awesome, soul-wrenching sobs of terror, dismay, and shame. At last she quieted and pulled gently away from him. He looked at her and saw in her eyes a sudden, fierce, cleansing anger.

"Oh, that bastard!" she cried, with withering vehemence. "Oh, that dirty, filthy bastard!"

Longarm almost laughed as he pulled her to him again and nodded in heartfelt agreement. "He is that, Stella. I agree. And he won't get away with it!"

"Do you promise?"

"I promise."

She began to cry then, softly, gently, and he let her. He held her and stroked her head while her tears dampened the front of his shirt. Certain now that Stella would be all right, he was immensely relieved. At last, when her weeping subsided, he kissed her lightly on the forehead.

She looked at him and blushed, and made a movement that affected him profoundly, as she brushed back an errant lock of hair from her forehead.

"It was a nightmare, wasn't it," she said.

"Yes."

"But I'm awake now."

Longarm nodded.

"I was such a fool," she said softly, bitterly. "I thought I was rid of him." She reached out then and took his arm. "He knows, Custis—about that letter, I mean. The one I sent to Washington."

"He found it?"

"He was waiting for me when I arrived back at the ranch. He saw it in my hand. I tried to keep it from him, but he took it away and read it."

"So now he's on his way to the Diamond T to show it to Paxman."

"Yes, I'm certain of it."

"That means Paxman knows who I am now, and why I'm up here."

"He had already suspected something," Stella pointed out. "That's why he kept sending Benton over to check on you."

Longarm nodded. "Well, this makes everything a mite simpler. Tomorrow I'll go see that sheriff and show him my credentials. Then we'll ride out to the Diamond T and demand that Paxman turn over Bob Loman to us. If he refuses, we'll have grounds for indicting the whole bunch."

"Sheriff Gulch? You'll ride out with him?"

"Yes." He smiled at the dismay on her face. "Don't be so surprised—though I must admit, he sure as hell didn't impress me much today when I saw him in action."

"I don't doubt it."

"What do you mean?"

"Custis, he's in with them! Paxman owns him, lock, stock, and barrel. It was Paxman who forced Gulch on us as sheriff. We had no one else to vote for. And the town constable, too. Paxman runs everything around here."

"I should have thought of that. No wonder Gulch was so anxious not to point the finger at Bob for Hoss's murder."

"Gulch was one of the first members of the Mullin Gang. According to Bob, he joined up with Mullin the same time Bob did."

120

Longarm took a deep breath and went to the window and looked down at the street below. He had blundered into the middle of an aroused bees' nest, like a grizzly poking through the honeycomb. Only he didn't have a grizzly's hide to protect him.

Chapter 8

Mullin was furious. Bob Loman had just burst in on him without warning, reciting an ugly, melancholy catalogue of butchery that could only mean trouble for Mullin and the rest of his gang.

Mullin did not know which was worse: the senseless murders Loman recounted or the glee with which he related them. Then had come the revelation concerning the letter Loman's wife Stella had sent to Washington. It was Bob Loman, then—Loman, and that woman he had married—who had brought that marshal up here, and it was the Mullin Gang the deputy marshal was looking for, after all. From what Mullin could gather from Loman's own botched, confused account, Loman had been wounded in the shoulder by either his foreman Abe or that marshal.

Mullin drew back in his swivel chair, edging away from the desk. For all he knew, Loman was probably dripping blood all over his desk as he stood panting over him, waiting for the approval he seemed to expect for bringing Mullin this appalling news. The poor fool was evidently convinced that by bringing in evidence of his wife's treachery, he was clearing himself, and would not really have to suffer Mullin's promised penalty for not clearing out.

It had not been easy for Mullin to mask his anger, and he was hoping he had been successful. Mullin had suffered the consequences of Loman's rank stupidity since he had first joined the gang, and now Mullin had reached the end of his patience. Indeed, at that very moment, Mullin was itching to get his hand on the Colt resting in his desk drawer. Nothing would please him more than to be able to blow a hole in Loman—a hole big enough for a bronc to buck through without touching. But he knew such an attempt would be fruitless. Close to him though Loman was standing, there was still a good likelihood that Mullin would miss.

In all the years of his blindness, this was the first time he cursed with all his soul at the darkness that had come between him and his fellow men.

"That's fine, Loman," he heard himself say. "You done right coming here. And I thank you for bringing me this news concerning that U. S. deputy. I have just one question."

"Sure, Jim. What is it?"

"Why did you tell your wife about the gang? Didn't I specifically warn you not to do that?"

"Sure, Jim. But I never thought she'd—"

"You mean, you never thought at all. That's what you mean, isn't it? You got yourself all liquored up one night and began boasting to her. Ain't that right?"

"Well, yes. But I didn't mean no harm, Jim!"

Mullin stifled his fury and forced himself to smile. He was well aware that it would not be wise for him to reveal to Loman what he really felt. Loman had already killed two men today—not to mention what he had done to his wife. Pushed to the limits by that damn fool, Gulch, and then seeing his wife panting after another man, Bob Loman had gone off the tracks. He'd snapped right in two, and all Mullin could do now was humor the son of a bitch.

"Just remindin' you, Bob," Mullin said gently. "Just remindin' you. But I guess I should've expected you'd want to tell Stella about yourself. Tell me, did you know she had written that letter?"

"I remembered her writing something that night, but I was pretty drunk at the time, and I just forgot about it. She never said a word about sending the letter, and I told her I'd never rat to the authorities."

Mullin said nothing.

"You believe me, don't you, Jim?"

"Of course I do. And I suppose you had to kill Abe. But what about Hoss? It ain't goin' to be easy to cover you for that one."

"It was that damn Gulch. I told you what he done.

Him and his card sharks wiped me out last night. They left me with nothing, then rubbed my nose in shit. I had no choice. Besides, Hoss treated me like dirt."

"And you ain't goin' to stand for that."

"Not no more, Jim." Loman's voice got edgy. "Not no more, I ain't."

"I don't blame you, Bob. Don't blame you one bit."

Footsteps approaching the ranch house came clearly to Mullin through the open window. He heard Benton's familiar boots tramping up onto the porch and breathed a little easier when he heard the housekeeper answering Benton's knock. He looked up past Loman as Benton knocked quickly on his door, then strode into the room.

"You wanted me, boss?" the foreman asked.

"Yes. Loman here has a slug in his shoulder. Have we got any extra bunks?"

"Not that I know of."

"How about that room in the horse barn? Bob'll have more peace and quiet in there, anyway. And while he's nursin' his wound, that's just what he'll need."

"Sure, boss."

"Thanks, Jim," Loman said warmly. "I really appreciate this."

"Not at all, Bob. You were one of the first men to join up with me, weren't you? You don't think I'd forget a thing like that, do you?"

"I guess not, Jim. But you sure sounded unfriendly yesterday."

126

"Today is another day, Bob. And don't forget, you've just brought me proof that this fellow Long is after me. For that warning, I am most grateful. I'll send my housekeeper in to clean out that wound of yours. She's very good at it. Then you can rest up. Tomorrow, first thing, we'll go after that federal marshal. How does that sound?"

"Just let me at him, Jim."

Mullin chuckled. "I'll see what I can do. Good night, Bob."

As Benton started to leave with Loman, Mullin called out to him. "After you get Bob settled in, send that new man, Pete Davis, in to see me. And you come with him."

"Sure, boss."

As soon as the door closed behind them, Mullin bellowed for his Indian housekeeper and told her to dig the slug out of Loman's wound, explaining to her where Loman would be laid up. She had been with Mullin ever since he began raising stagecoaches and had become as expert as an army surgeon when it came to probing for slugs. She grunted assent and pulled the door shut.

A moment later Mullin heard hoofbeats clattering in through the gate. The horse was coming fast, the rider obviously in a big hurry. Whoever it was pulled up outside his window and tramped up onto the porch.

"Who's there?" Mullin bellowed out the open window.

"It's Gulch, Jim," came the response.

The housekeeper answered the outside door. Mullin turned in his chair and was staring blindly at his office door when Gulch knocked once and let himself in.

As Gulch approached his desk, Mullin said, "If it's about Hoss's murder, I'm way ahead of you. Loman was just in here. He's stayin' at the Diamond T for now."

"You mean he's here? Now?"

"Yes, he's here. He's probably bled all over my desk."

"Who wounded him?"

"I'm not sure. Neither is he. Maybe Abe, or that marshal."

Gulch shook his head. "That stupid son of a bitch. I tell you, Jim, Loman's gone crazy. Plumb crazy."

"I know it. The worm has turned. And for that I hold you partly responsible, Gulch."

"Me?"

"Loman told me about you and your buddies cleaning him out last night, then kicking him out of the saloon. He was a desperate man when he woke up today. I'd told him I'd kill him if he didn't clear out of this territory. I wanted to be rid of him, but your greed ruined my plan. Loman panicked when he realized he was broke this morning. Now we have to deal with the result."

"Sorry, Jim. But Loman made such a nice punching bag."

"There's something else, something I gather you don't know."

"What's that?"

"Loman has just told me what that deputy U. S. marshal is doing up here. He's looking for an informant, one who would turn us all in for a chance at a government pardon. That marshal is looking for the Mullin Gang, Gulch—and it was Loman's wife who talked Loman into the idea."

"Loman? *He's* goin' to give evidence? You mean he's goin' to testify against *us?*"

"Not now, he isn't. His wife sent a letter offering his services as an informer without letting him know she'd sent it. The letter is on my desk here, I believe." He patted the top of the desk until he came to it. Then he handed it up to the sheriff.

"Can you read, Sheriff?"

"Course I can."

"Good. Read it aloud to me."

When the sheriff finished reading it, he dropped the letter back onto Mullin's desk and swore softly. "Well, I'll be damned!"

"We have to get this marshal, Gulch. And we've got to move fast. Before this night is out. Do you know where he might be now?"

"Sure. He's in Dun Creek with Stella Loman at the hotel. The doc just got through visitin' her. Seems Loman really worked her over, and it was this marshal who rescued her."

Mullin frowned. "Then she's not dead. Loman was hoping he'd burned her alive."

"Well, she ain't dead, and that U. S. marshal is taking very good care of her in his hotel room."

"Then we're in luck. The way it looks now, you're

going to be riding back to Dun Creek with a dead man and a warrant for the arrest of deputy U. S. marshal Custis Long."

"A warrant? What for?"

"The murder of Stella's husband, Bob Loman. And I wouldn't be surprised if an aroused citizenry lynched the murdering bastard before the day was out. Bob Loman had a lot of friends in these parts."

"Bob Loman?" Gulch asked, incredulous.

The office door opened and Mullin heard two men entering. He swung his head away from the sheriff. "That you, Benton?"

"It's me boss—and I got Pete with me, like you said."

"Come closer, Pete. I have a job for you. You might say it will serve as your initiation. You willing?"

"Sure, Mr. Paxman."

"Then listen, and listen carefully."

Bob Loman put down the dime novel he was reading and looked up as Pete Davis entered his room. Davis had to turn his body a little to get his enormous shoulders through the doorway.

"Hi, Pete," Loman said.

"How you feelin'?" asked Pete, studying Loman closely, without concern and without compassion.

"Better. Much better."

The Indian housekeeper had worked the slug out of the fleshy part of Loman's shoulder with little difficulty, then washed out the wound. Though it burned fiercely now, Loman knew it was clean and that he would soon be as good as new, and once again a member in good standing of the Mullin Gang. He felt like someone who had just come home after a long and miserable journey through unfriendly country. The madness that had ignited him these past few hours was slipping away from him like an unclean garment.

"That's good," said Pete. He turned a rickety wooden chair around and sat astride it, his arms folded onto the back of it. "Got your own private room here, huh? Ain't you the lucky one."

"I wasn't so lucky this morning. I woke up in an alley alongside a shithouse. My luck's changing, Pete. Finally."

"Glad to hear it. What you readin'?"

Loman lifted the cover of the book so Pete could read it. He did. "The History of the James Boys, huh? Is it good?"

Loman grinned. "They ain't caught any of 'em yet."

"And they never will."

"And they won't never catch the Mullin Gang, neither. You're lucky to join up with such a famous gang, I can tell you."

"I know. And I owe it all to that big son of a bitch who's been putting it to your wife," Pete said.

Loman's face went scarlet. "I wish you wouldn't talk like that about her."

"Hell, you burned her, didn't you?"

131

"Yeah, but I don't like you talking about her like that."

Pete sighed. "Well, I guess that means you and I will just never get along." He took out his sixgun.

Loman looked at the gun in Pete's hand, his eyes widening in sudden panic. "Hey, what the hell are you doin' with that?"

"Shut up. Just shut up."

Pete took the folded blanket resting on the foot of Loman's bed and hefted it. Yes, it was thick enough, he concluded, as he thrust the muzzle of his Colt into it.

"Pete!" Loman cried. "Put down that gun!"

Pete just smiled.

Loman started to get out of bed. Pete withdrew the gun from the blanket and struck Loman across the right temple with it, the barrel opening a livid gash all the way to Loman's cheekbone. Loman crumpled back onto his cot, still conscious, but groggy.

He groaned slightly as Pete poked the sixgun under the sheet covering Loman, then jammed the muzzle into the soft flesh of Loman's stomach. Reaching back for the blanket, he crushed the blanket down over his gun hand and pulled the trigger. The detonation filled the room with a muffled *whomp*, but there was little if any reverberation. Pete withdrew his Colt from under the blanket and holstered it. Then he carefully folded the blanket to hide the hole in it and placed it neatly down on the foot of Loman's cot.

Then, without a backward glance, he let himself out of the room and strode from the barn.

• • •

Longarm was trying to get comfortable in the chair by his bed. Not long before, Stella had lapsed finally into an exhausted sleep. He had dropped off himself once or twice, but each time the difficulty of getting his long frame comfortable in the cramped chair had awakened him. He was considering getting into bed beside Stella when he heard stumbling footsteps approaching the door. He came alert at once and stood up.

"Custis!" came a hoarse, drunken whisper from the other side of the door. It was Doc Gilmore.

Longarm went to the door and pulled it open. The doctor staggered in. Longarm closed the door behind him.

"She's fine, Doc," Longarm said. "There's no need for you to worry about her. She's come out of it just fine."

"She has, but *you* won't."

"What're you talkin' about, Doc?"

"The sheriff's just rode in from the Diamond T. There'll be Diamond T riders coming in after him in a few minutes. At the moment, Sheriff Gulch is drawing up a warrant for your arrest."

"My arrest?"

"Yes. For killing Bob Loman."

"Hell, I just winged him."

"Nevertheless, he's dead. Gulch has already alerted the undertaker. I was at the back table in the saloon when Gulch came after him. He made no secret of what he was about."

133

"It's a frame. It won't hold up for ten minutes."

"Of course it won't. But ten minutes is all Gulch needs. He'll clap you in jail and there'll be a lynching party before the night's out."

Longarm moved swiftly over to the corner, and snatched up his rifle and the rest of his gear. "I'd better get moving."

"And you don't have much time!"

"Stay here, Doc. Look after Stella. You got a gun?"

The doctor pulled a Smith and Wesson out of his belt. "It's fully loaded," he said.

"Anything to drink?"

He patted a hip flask.

"Good luck, then. And don't be afraid to use that gun if you have to. They just might come after Stella, too. She knows what I do—and what you know now, as well. Jim Paxman is the leader of the Mullin Gang."

"I was wondering how come such a poor cattleman needed so many gun-toting ranch hands, not one of whom knows a thing about running cattle."

"You don't have to wonder any more. Don't leave this room until daylight, and when you do, send a telegram to the U. S. Marshal's office in Denver. You'll know what to tell them."

"Indeed, I will, Marshal."

Longarm glanced over at Stella. She was still sound asleep. He left the room and pulled the door shut behind him. He found the back stairs and descended them to the alley, then darted out from behind the hotel across to the livery stable.

He had just finished saddling up when he heard

horsemen storming into town. The Diamond T riders.
As he mounted up he heard them clattering to a halt
in the street in front of the hotel. Ducking his head
low, he rode out of the stable—and right at them.

When they saw Longarm bearing down on them,
they pulled their horses around in some confusion.
Benton was in their midst. He shouted something that
got lost in the clatter. Then the riders started to break
left, others went to the right, clawing for their side-
arms as they did so. But before their weapons could
clear leather, Longarm ran the nearest one down and
clubbed the next one from his saddle, then cut down
an alley and up a side street.

In a moment he was on his way out of town. He
did not need to look back to know that Benton and
the other riders were pouring after him. The shouting
of the riders and the thunder of their hooves told him
that.

The moon was high, and he was riding due north.
A distant line of peaks and misshapen bluffs shoul-
dered into the night sky ahead of him.

As good a terrain as any to lose the Diamond T
riders on his tail.

Chapter 9

A mile or so out of town, Longarm lost his pursuers while cutting through a patch of timber. But, cresting a ridge a little after dawn, he saw the dogged Diamond T riders still pounding after him.

He grunted in grim satisfaction, stayed on the ridge until they caught sight of him, then kept on into the rugged foothills. He was careful to leave tracks. If he found his horse riding for an extended distance over exceptionally hard ground, he would look for a soft spot to ride through as soon as possible after leaving the hard ground. He kept up a steady pace, but did not punish the black, stopping frequently to rest and water him.

At mid-morning he pulled up before the badlands,

studying the terrain ahead of him carefully. At last his eyes caught a formation that would be right for the plan he was conceiving. He spurred his black on into the badlands. Soon he was well inside them, keeping to as straight a path as possible through the narrow defiles and arroyos. Whenever possible, he chose to pass under overhanging ridges or close to the foot of the sheer rock walls.

At midday he camped by a clear stream that trickled out from behind a rock formation at the foot of a butte. In the butte's welcome shade, he off-saddled the black, peeled off the saddle blanket, and rubbed the animal down. Then, using his saddle for a pillow, he relaxed beside the cool stream, his hobbled black cropping the lush grass growing in the stream's shallows. Closing his eyes, he rested but did not sleep.

He kept track of the sun carefully, and after about an hour he saddled the black and rode on, this time traveling up the bed of the stream. He was looking for hard ground to emerge onto . . . either that or an extensive outcropping of cap rock. He found a ledge finally and guided the black onto it. Forcing the animal to walk so as not to chip the stone with his shoes, Longarm kept going until he saw a thick stand of lodgepole pines crowding the ledge off to his right. He rode carefully up to the edge of the timber, then guided the black off into a clump of junipers bordering the pines, kept to the brush for a quarter of a mile or so, then entered the pines.

He kept in the timber for a mile or so, gaining altitude steadily. At last he came out onto a gray sandstone ridge that ran for a considerable distance along the topmost elevations of the badlands. It was this formation he had spotted from the foothills. He had been keeping it in sight from below as he rode deeper and deeper into the badlands.

Now he rode back along the rocky spine, retracing the course he had just followed—but this time from a much higher vantage point. Pushing his black to the limit now, he reached the end of the ridge with at least six hours of sun left in the sky. Tethering his horse in a clump of stunted cedars, he crept well out onto a narrow ledge which gave him an unobstructed view of the rolling foothills he had left behind him earlier that day.

Peering into the shimmering distance, Longarm saw nothing. Since he had caught no sign of any pursuers as he traveled back along the sandstone ridge, he was beginning to wonder if the Diamond T riders had given up. But this hardly seemed likely. In order to cover his operation, Mullin's men would have to deal with Longarm swiftly. And that meant they would have to keep after him without letup until they cornered him and finished him off.

At last Longarm's instincts were rewarded. His eye picked out the tiny figures of five riders strung out in single file as they rode along the crest of a distant foothill. Longarm smiled. They were still on his trail— and as long as they were, Benton and the Diamond T riders would not be threatening Stella.

There were five of them.

Longarm watched the oncoming riders for a while

longer, noting that they were driving their mounts hard in an effort to overtake him and seemed to be having no difficulty at all in following his trail.

Longarm climbed off the ledge and hurried back to his mount. Taking just his lariat and sixgun, Longarm returned to the ledge, then began to make his way down the steep canyon wall to its floor below, moving with infinite care to see that he did not dislodge a single pebble. At last he reached the floor of the canyon and darted out from its mouth to a spot he`had noted when first he entered the badlands—a confusing maze of house-sized boulders, a shiny obsidian in color, that seemed to have grown out of the canyon floor. He slipped in among the boulders and hunkered down to wait.

The lead rider was the Diamond T foreman. He rode with his eyes watching the ground intently. As he clopped past Longarm and into the canyon, Benton leaned back in his saddle and yelled to his straggling riders to close up.

They urged their laboring mounts after him with little enthusiasm. They were well strung out by this time, the last rider in the file a good two hundred yards back. Longarm let them all ride on past him into the canyon after Benton. It was the last rider he wanted, and as this one passed Longarm and entered the narrow canyon, Longarm strode quickly out from behind the boulder, his lariat held ready. This last rider was now the only one in sight, the rest having disappeared into the shadows of the arroyo well ahead of him.

Longarm had already pocketed his spurs. With quick, loping strides, he closed to within twenty yards of the trailing rider, shook out his lariat, and with one quick toss dropped its loop over the rider's head. A vicious, snapping tug closed it about the rider's throat. Able to utter only a strangling cry, the man was pulled violently backward off his horse.

For a moment Longarm was afraid the horse would spook and take off down the canyon after the others. But the animal reared only once and then, finding his saddle suddenly light, pulled up to glance back at his fallen rider. By that time Longarm had reached the Diamond T rider and loosened the rope from around his neck.

The man had not moved since striking the ground. The rope had snapped his neck, killing him almost instantly. Longarm flung the coiled rope over his shoulder. He took the rider by his boots, dragged him to the edge of the canyon, and dropped him behind a boulder. He did not want the vultures to advertise his presence too soon.

Then Longarm went back for the horse, pulled the saddle off, turned him about, and sent him back out of the canyon with a sharp slap to his rump. With almost welcome relief, his tail high, the horse galloped off toward the grass-covered foothills.

It was not long after this, as Longarm expected, that a Diamond T rider galloped back through the canyon to find out what had happened to their drag. Longarm had lugged the dead man's saddle out of the canyon and dropped it to one side of the canyon entrance, close in under the rock wall beside a large boulder. Clattering out of the canyon, the rider spotted the saddle almost at once and flung off his horse to investigate. His sixgun was in his hand as he knelt by the saddle to examine its markings.

Longarm stepped out of the shadows behind him and spoke quietly. "Drop it, mister."

This hardcase had no overpowering desire to spend his declining years in a rocking chair. With a violent oath, he spun about, his sixgun blazing. His first round went wild; his second took Longarm's hat off his head. Longarm crunched the barrel of his sixgun down on the side of the man's head, just above the ear. The man sagged to the ground, his face up, his breath coming in short, painful gasps, a thin trickle of blood streaming from his left temple.

The two shots would bring the three others—fast.

Longarm slung this second rider's gunbelt over his shoulder, tossed the fellow's sixgun away, then began his scramble back up to the ridge overhead. He was better than halfway to it when the remaining three riders, with Benton in the lead, clattered out of the mouth of the canyon below him and discovered their fallen comrade. They leaped from their horses, guns drawn. It didn't take them long to find Longarm's tracks. One of them followed the trail to the rocks and then to the side of the bluff, Longarm climbing swiftly higher with each passing moment.

The Diamond T gunslick ran back away from the cliff to get a better view of the slope. Longarm tried to keep out of sight as he climbed, but it was impossible. With a sudden shout, the gunslick pointed up at Longarm. The other two raced back and began pumping lead at Longarm, but by this time he was out of range. Holstering their guns, the Diamond T riders raced for the foot of the bluff to follow him up.

Longarm climbed swiftly now, without care, perfectly willing to set off small avalanches of rocks, sand, and debris that just might dislodge his pursuers. He reached the ridge, raced back to the cedars, and mounted his black. Just as he put the black on down the ridge, a Diamond T rider climbed into view and began firing after him. Pulling up and hauling his Winchester from its scabbard, Longarm levered a cartridge into the firing chamber, swung around in his saddle, and with cool, thoughtful deliberation squeezed off a shot. The Diamond T rider buckled, staggered back a few steps, then toppled from the ridge.

When Benton and the single remaining Diamond T rider reached the crest of the ridge, Longarm had vanished.

Benton and his companion had built their campfire against a rock face and had then carefully fashioned two dummy sleepers out of boulders and blankets, setting them a small distance from the fire. As the dancing light played upon the still forms, they looked surprisingly lifelike. The only thing wrong with the scheme was that Longarm had expected just such a threadbare deception.

Crouched atop an overhanging ledge almost directly above the campfire, Longarm knew that somewhere—halfway up the slope above the dummy figures, perhaps—Benton and his partner were waiting in the darkness for Longarm to make his move.

Longarm made himself comfortable on the ledge and waited until the fire had died down some before tossing a cartridge from the cartridge belt he'd borrowed into the fire. The sound of the shell clicking against the rocks enclosing the fire could be heard dimly from his perch. Longarm knew the two men waiting in the darkness could hear it as well, but this did not mean they knew what it was they had heard.

Not sure the cartridge had remained within reach of the campfire, Longarm waited a few moments, then tossed down three more. Only when he noticed a slight disturbance in the embers was he sure that one of them had reached the fire. He waited a while longer, then tossed down two more. Satisfied, he stood up on the ledge with his Winchester tucked into his shoulder, a fresh cartridge already cranked into the firing chamber, the safety off.

For an uncomfortably long period of time it seemed his ruse was not going to work as the fire continued to burn itself out. Finally it was just a single guttering flame surrounded by an irregular star of fading embers.

Abruptly, the fireworks began.

In quick succession the embers were blasted apart

as first one, then another cartridge exploded. The sound of the bullets ricocheting off the surrounding rock faces filled the night. And then a third cartridge went off. All this within the space of four, perhaps five, seconds.

Suddenly a dark figure bolted from behind a clump of scrub pine above the campfire, his sixgun blazing as he fired at someone he thought he saw to the right of the fire. Longarm lifted his Winchester, aimed just behind the gun flashes, and squeezed. The dark figure buckled and tumbled headfirst down the slope toward the exploding fire.

At once, Longarm flattened himself on the ledge as another flash from higher up the slope sent a slug whistling past his ear. Another round followed the first, striking the lip of the ledge on which he lay, causing an explosion of rock shards to erupt in his face. He looked quickly away, then sighted at the flashes and squeezed the trigger. He heard the slug ricochet off rock. Then came another flash from a different position on the slope. A second round whispered past his right shoulder.

Cautiously, Longarm backed off the ledge, dodged through a cleft in the rock, and climbed to the ridge to his tethered horse. Dropping his Winchester into its scabbard, he swung into his saddle and rode off, grateful for what moonlight still remained.

Early that morning, before the sunlight had reached the floor of the badlands, Longarm watched a single Diamond T rider leaving the badlands, his right arm in a makeshift sling, his body hunched forward over the pommel. Dismounting, Longarm left his black and climbed down closer to the floor of the canyon to get a better view of the rider. It was not Benton. It was his remaining partner. This was the one he had winged the night before. Longarm climbed back up the slope, remounted, and headed for higher ground.

He had hoped it was Benton he had winged above the campfire, though good sense had told him that Benton would not have spooked so easily and started shooting at shadows like that. No, it was Benton who had driven Longarm off the ledge.

Which meant Benton was not running. He was remaining in the badlands, determined to bring Longarm down. By this time, Longarm realized, the Diamond T foreman had now acquired the same advantages Longarm had used so skillfully earlier—surprise and a knowledge of the terrain. Aware of this, Longarm rode now with great care, his eyes inspecting every bush, every overhanging ledge.

It did not come as a complete surprise, then, when he rounded an odd-shaped boulder high above the badlands and found himself facing Benton. There was a grim smile on Benton's unshaven face as he aimed his rifle's muzzle at Longarm. Longarm acted instinctively. Even as the Diamond T's foreman tightened his finger on the trigger, he flung himself forward over the head of his black onto Benton's horse.

The rifle fired as he leaped, and Longarm felt a slug tear through his sleeve. But he paid no attention as he caught the bridle of Benton's horse and yanked the animal's head brutally around as he fell between the two horses. The horse reared in sudden panic, in a desperate effort to pull its head free of Longarm's cruel grasp. As he did so, he unseated Benton, who tumbled backward off his horse.

The man came down heavily on his back, his rifle flying from his grasp. Longarm flung himself on him. The two struggling men rolled over and over, hammering each other with bloody, chopping blows, until at last Longarm managed to stun the Diamond T foreman with a sledging blow to the point of his chin. He stood up then and drew his Colt. But as he steadied himself to shoot, Benton snatched up a fist-sized rock and hurled it with murderous accuracy at Longarm's head.

The rock struck Longarm flush on the forehead. He felt as if he had ridden into the side of a mountain. His Colt slipping from his fingers, he staggered backward. The ground slammed into his back, his head coming down with cruel force upon the rocky trail. Lights exploded in his skull. His previous injury had rendered his skull unusually sensitive, and he felt his senses reeling. He tried to open his eyes, but all he could manage was a tiny flicker of the eyelids. Yet it was enough for him to see through a reddish haze the panting, grinning figure of the foreman, the grim smile on his face as he hastily went back for his rifle.

Your derringer! Longarm told himself. *Use it!*

Almost without willing it, he felt his hand clawing the derringer out of his vest pocket. He saw the surprise on the foreman's face as he turned back to Longarm and saw the ugly little pistol in Longarm's hand. Then Longarm felt first one, then another barrel belch fire. Both rounds planted neat holes in Benton's dirty shirtfront.

The foreman staggered back, then fought to stay on his feet. He tried to raise his rifle and fire down at Longarm, but the effort was too much for him and he crumpled face down. Longarm tried to roll away, but was unable to move far enough as the rifle clattered to the ground and the dead man collapsed forward onto him. Still partially paralyzed, Longarm's limbs would not respond to his efforts to pull himself free of the foreman's dead weight. He lay back, cursing, until at last enough strength returned to enable him to roll out from under his grisly burden.

He pulled himself painfully erect, his head still rocking with pain, retrieved his Colt, and caught the hanging reins of his black about ten feet away. As he pulled himself into the saddle, he realized he needed a place where he could lick his wounds.

That was when he thought of Clem Hardin's Lazy H ranch.

Chapter 10

Longarm came within sight of the Lazy H late that afternoon. He was still groggy from that crack on the skull and by the time he rode into the ranch's compound, he was in no condition to dismount gracefully. He dimly remembered hanging on foolishly to the saddle while Randy Walls hurried over to help him down.

Then he was looking into Hardin's concerned face as he was helped inside the ranch house. He did not remember passing out, but it was dark when he regained consciousness, lying face up on a horsehair sofa in the living room.

The only light came from a kerosene lamp on a corner table. Hardin, his white thatch of hair strikingly visible in the dim room, was sitting in an armchair near one window, watching him. As Longarm stirred and tried to sit up, Hardin called out to his housekeeper, then got up from his chair and walked over to the sofa.

"Anything I can do for you?" he asked.

"Yeah," Longarm managed, sitting up slowly and rubbing the back of his head. "Join me in a smoke— if I have any cheroots left."

Longarm's frock coat had been hung over the back of a chair nearby. Hardin plucked it off the chair and handed it to him.

"Join me," said Longarm, taking out his last two cheroots and handing one to Hardin.

"Don't mind if I do," Hardin said.

Hardin produced a match and lit both cheroots. Then he pulled a chair over and sat down alongside Longarm. "You want to tell me about it?" he asked.

"About what?"

"Your one-man massacre of the Diamond T."

"You mean I got them all?"

"Not yet, but you sure as hell put a dent in their numbers."

"You know about it, then?"

"After you showed up here, I rode into Dun Creek to get the doctor. I couldn't find him. And no one knew where the sheriff was, either. But I heard talk in Steadman's. Hoss and Bob Loman were buried today. Paxman and the rest of his riders showed up for the funeral, and one of the Diamond T riders let it out that the only rider who's come back so far from chasing you has a broken arm."

"And he's the only one who'll be coming back," Longarm said.

"That's what everyone figured."

The housekeeper hustled in, carrying a tray containing a bottle of bourbon and two large glasses. She put the tray down on a table beside the sofa, then went back out.

"How do you feel?" Hardin asked.

Longarm reached back gingerly and felt his skull. There was a lump, but his head was no longer as sensitive, and the headache that had threatened to cause all the lights to go out was now but a faint memory. "Much better, thanks," he said.

"You feel up to a drink?"

Longarm grinned. "Let's give it a try."

Hardin filled both glasses halfway up and handed Longarm his drink. Longarm downed the bourbon gratefully. It braced him and at the same time reminded him how famished he was. He suggested to Hardin that some food would be nice to help settle the bourbon, since he hadn't eaten in twenty-four hours. Hardin brought his housekeeper back with another shout and told her to fix Longarm some grub.

Longarm thanked Hardin, then asked, "Did I hear you say you couldn't find Doc Gilmore?"

"That's right."

"I don't like that."

"Why?"

"I left him with Stella Loman. All he had with him to protect her and himself was a Smith and Wesson. I hope he didn't have to use it."

"Why would they be in danger?"

"Paxman has to kill her as well as me," Longarm told him.

Hardin frowned in astonishment. "You want to try that on me one more time? Why in hell would Paxman want to kill you and Stella Loman?"

Longarm told Hardin all he knew concerning Paxman's true identity, including Stella's letter, and explained how it had brought Longarm to Dun Creek looking for the informant who might lead him to the Mullin Gang.

When he had finished, Hardin shook his head. He was so agitated by what Longarm had just told him that he began pacing. "In other words, Jim Paxman is really Jim Mullin! And those hardcases on his spread are gunslicks waiting to pull another job."

"You having trouble believing that?" Longarm asked.

"On the contrary. For the first time, things around here are beginning to make sense. Now I know how that spread has prospered without taking care of their fences or their stock. Hell, they haven't even participated in a roundup now for more than two years. Myself and the other ranchers nearby just figured Paxman gave up because he lost his sight. I see now that if that was part of the reason, it sure as hell wasn't the only one."

The housekeeper returned to announce that food was ready. Longarm walked into the kitchen and found waiting for him a well-singed steak, baked potatoes covered with rich gravy, and thick slices of homemade bread with strawberry preserves. He ate with unabashed greed, topping off the meal with steaming cups of coffee.

Hardin had finished his cheroot by that time. He leaned back in his chair and joined Longarm in a cup of coffee.

"So what now?" he asked.

"You also said that when you went in for the doctor, no one knew where the sheriff was. That right?"

Hardin nodded.

"I suppose you realize that Mullin owns the sheriff?"

Hardin nodded. "We all knew that from the beginning. Paxman has wielded considerable clout around here since he first bought up the Diamond T five years ago—principally because no one else wanted to bother with that sort of thing."

"The constable is also in Mullin's pocket, I gather."

Hardin nodded fatalistically.

"Then maybe you can understand why I'm worried about Stella and the doc."

"I guess I can."

"So I'm riding in to Dun Creek to find them. Now."

"Fine. And I think I'll join you," Hardin said.

"That's not necessary."

"I know that. But I am still going with you."

Longarm got up from his chair, smiling. "All right. Suit yourself. But that black of mine must be worn out by now."

"I'll have a fresh horse saddled for you at once."

Hardin got up quickly and hurried from the kitchen. Watching him go, Longarm realized that for the first time since he had first met the cattleman, the big, craggy fellow no longer seemed on the verge of cracking. It seemed that he had been able to put the death of his daughter behind him. Perhaps it was the prospect of doing something positive, of making things happen instead of letting things happen to him.

It was because Longarm sensed this that he made no effort at all to dissuade Hardin from riding in to Dun Creek with him.

Longarm and Hardin were in sight of Dun Creek's lamplit streets when they heard a rider behind them. They swung around in their saddles to see Randy Walls overtaking them.

"Soon's I figured what was up," he said, pulling up alongside them, "I took after you."

"Damn it, Randy," protested Hardin. "You'll likely get your head blown off."

"Knew you'd put up a fuss. That's why I waited this long to show myself."

He grinned at Longarm, who smiled right back at him.

Longarm guided his mount over to the water tower and pulled up in its shadow. He waited for Hardin and Randy to pull up beside him.

"You two go into Steadman's for a drink and find out what's going on," Longarm suggested. "Keep an eye out for the sheriff and the constable. I'll slip into the hotel from the rear and check to see if Stella and the doc are still in my room."

"A lot of good we'll be doing downstairs in the saloon," Hardin protested.

"That's right," said Randy. "We ought to go up with you."

"I'm not finished," Longarm told them. "While I'm up there, get two horses from the livery and bring them around to the alley in the rear of the hotel. We all might have to get out of this town in a hurry. But don't go into the hotel yourself unless I need you."

"How in hell are we supposed to know that?" demanded Randy.

"You'll know when you hear it."

Randy sent a black dart of tobacco juice from the corner of his mouth. "Just don't outsmart yerself, like you did the last time, Marshal."

Longarm said nothing as the two men pulled away from him and continued on into Dun Creek. Longarm watched them for a second or two; then he turned his mount toward the stream that looped Dun Creek and the wooded hills beyond. His intention was to enter the town from the rear and keep to the back alleys until he reached the hotel.

He encountered no opposition slipping through the hotel's rear door and moving up the back steps, but when he reached the second floor and peered down the hallway, he saw a thin rake of a fellow sitting in a chair with his back to Longarm's room, a rifle cradled in his arms. Longarm recognized the man. He was the town constable.

Longarm ducked back out of sight. He thought a minute, then took out his Colt, checked to make sure its safety was on, then deliberately dropped the revolver to the floor. It thumped loudly. Longarm quickly picked it up and listened. He heard nothing.

He waited a moment longer, then peered carefully around the corner. The constable was no longer sitting with his chair tipped back. He was peering in Longarm's direction. Longarm pulled his head back out of sight, cleared his throat loudly, and dropped his gun a second time.

This time he heard the constable get to his feet and start to walk slowly, cautiously, down the hallway toward him. He did not walk far before he halted uncertainly. In a hoarse whisper he croaked, "Anyone there?"

Longarm straightened up and flattened himself against the wall. He held his revolver by the barrel. Again he cleared his throat.

The constable took a few steps closer. A foot from the corner, he pulled up again.

"Damn it!" he whispered. "Who's there?"

Longarm tapped the wall behind him twice with the butt of his revolver. In an agony of indecision, the constable pulled himself together and stepped around the corner. Longarm grabbed him by the arm and yanked him all the way around. Before he could utter anything more than a barely audible yelp, Longarm clubbed him on the top of the head. As the town constable collapsed to the floor like an empty grain sack, Longarm snatched his rifle, catching it before it crashed to the floor.

Then he peered around the corner. The hallway was now empty. He moved swiftly down the hall and paused in front of the door, then placed his ear against it. He could not be sure, but he thought he heard Stella talking softly and angrily to someone. Longarm kept his ear against the door, and this time heard a harsh voice he recognized as Sheriff Gulch's telling her to shut up.

Longarm sat down in the chair the constable had vacated and leaned it back against the door. He did it forcefully, the back of the chair cracking the door sharply. Then he did it again.

"Skinner!" Gulch cried. "Get that chair back away from the door!"

With his fingers firmly closed about the grips of his Colt, Longarm folded his arms, brought his chair forward, then back against the door again. This time, as it crunched into the door, Longarm uttered something inarticulate at the same time. He heard Gulch swear and start toward the door.

Longarm pulled his hat down over his eyes and leaned forward in the chair a split second before the exasperated sheriff pulled the door open behind him. Angrily, Gulch reached down to grab the shoulder of the man he thought was the town constable. At the same time Longarm reached up with his left hand, caught Gulch behind his collar, and stood up, flinging the burly man over his shoulder. The astonished Gulch struck the floor on his back, heavily. Before he could shake himself alert and draw his iron, Longarm aimed his .44 calmly down at him and smiled.

"Take it easy, Gulch."

Stella's sudden shout came from the room behind him. "Custis! Watch out!"

Longarm spun in time to see the door darken as a Diamond T ranch hand filled it. He had a Colt in his hand and was about to use it. A revolver's detonation came from behind him. The slug caught him full in the back and rammed him across the corridor into the wall. He struck it head on, then collapsed face down.

Longarm looked back at the sheriff. Gulch had drawn his own weapon. Both men fired at the same time. Longarm's slug caught Gulch in his face, turning one eye socket into a rapidly expanding hole. The slug meant for Longarm struck the ceiling behind him.

Turning away, Longarm stepped over the other one and glanced into the room. The doc had a pleased expression on his face, and in his hand a smoking Smith and Wesson. Stella was bound hand and foot on the bed.

As Longarm hurried into the room, the doctor shoved the weapon into the pocket of his frock coat and began untying Stella's hands.

"Nice shot, Doc," said Longarm as he began to untie Stella's ankles. "How the hell did you manage it?"

Gilmore grinned happily across the bed at Longarm. "They never thought to pat me down to see if I

158

carried a gun. I saved it up for just the right moment."

"You did," Longarm agreed. He glanced at the woman. "You all right, Stella?"

"Not until I get out of here," she told him, furious. "This hotel is crawling with Paxman's men."

"Mullin must've emptied out hell when he recruited his riders," agreed the doc as he helped Stella to her feet. "You got in here, Long. But have you got a way out?"

"I have two horses waiting downstairs."

"Then let's go!"

It was impossible for Stella to move fast. The circulation had been cut off in her ankles. Longarm lifted her in his arms and followed Doc Gilmore down the hall. Glancing back a moment before he turned the corner leading to the back stairs, he saw the heads of two men swarming up the front stairs to check on all the gunfire.

Randy and Hardin had secured the two horses. They were waiting in the alley. But both men were some distance away, standing with guns drawn at opposite corners of the hotel building. When they saw Longarm and the doc boiling out of the rear door, they raced back to their horses.

"We better move fast!" Randy called to Longarm. "There were two Diamond T riders in the hotel lobby."

Longarm lifted Stella onto one of the two saddled horses and thrust the reins into her hands. "Can you ride?"

"Get out of my way, Marshal," she said grimly. "And watch!"

Longarm swung into his saddle and raced off down the alley, the rest following. He cut across the stream just outside of town and led them into the wooded hills that flanked the town. It was the way he had entered town not long before, and when the five riders pulled up and looked back, they saw the two Diamond T riders racing down the main street, heading in the other direction.

Hardin spoke up. "No one paid much attention to Randy and me when we rode in a little while ago, so I don't think anyone has connected us with this hotel business. But there's no need for us to take any chances. I suggest you let me lead the way back to the Lazy H. I'll approach it from the north."

"Just lead the way," Longarm said.

It was close to midnight when they arrived back at Hardin's ranch. Once inside the living room, Stella and the doc told them of their ordeal. After Paxman— or Mullin, as the doctor was now referring to him— rode into town for the funerals of Bob Loman and Hoss, he let Gulch take him up to Stella's room.

At the time, the doctor had been downstairs in the lobby, seeing about having a meal sent up to Stella. He hurried up the stairs after Mullin and found him standing before Stella, interrogating her, a powerfully built, barn-sized bodyguard alongside him.

"Mullin threw my letter back at me," Stella explained. "Bob must have given it to him. He asked me if I had written it. I told him I had."

"What was his response to that?" Hardin asked.

"He told me I was a fool to have sent the letter, that Bob had been lying about him. He insisted that he was not the leader of any gang of bank robbers."

"And of course you believed him."

"I did not," she said, "but I pretended to be thinking it over."

"She played it real cute," Doc Gilmore said, breaking in. "She said if she had made a mistake, she would most certainly apologize."

"I didn't fool him all that much," Stella went on ruefully. "He left, but when the doctor and I tried to get out of the room, we found it guarded by one of his men."

"We knew things were really going bad," the doctor went on, "when Mullin rode out of town that night and Sheriff Gulch came up to our room and tied Stella up and told us that we were Gulch's prisoners. He said we were accessories after the fact of Bob Loman's murder."

"And of course," said Stella, "*you* were the murderer, Custis."

"And we were the bait," said the doctor. "They knew you'd come back for Stella, if not for me. I don't know what Mullin promised Gulch if he nailed you, Long, but Gulch was sure anxious to take you."

"And so were the others," said Stella.

Longarm glanced at the doctor. "And I guess you never got the chance to send that telegram."

"Sorry, Longarm."

Longarm looked back at Gilmore. Something the doctor had said earlier still bothered him. "This bodyguard you mentioned, the one you saw standing beside Mullin when he was questioning Stella. You said he was a big man. How big was he?"

"He had powerful, broad shoulders, as broad as yours, I'd say. He was certainly big around, but solid all the way."

"He was frightening," said Stella. "He looked so fierce."

Longarm frowned and looked at Hardin, but Hardin had already caught on to what Longarm was thinking. He stepped closer to Stella.

"Describe what he looked like," he told her. "His hair, his eyes."

Stella did as good a job as she could. When she was through, the doctor added a few more details. When they had finished, Longarm and Hardin both knew they had found Connie Hardin's murderer, and the man who had almost succeeded in killing Longarm. Randy had recognized the description as well.

"Well, now," said Longarm. "I should have figured it. A man like Pete Davis would sure as hell find a home with Mullin." He glanced at Hardin. "It looks like we've got our work cut out for us."

"When do we move on him?" Hardin asked.

"As soon as possible. When Mullin sees how things are going, there's a good chance he'll more than likely decide to clear out—and fast."

"We going to move out tonight?" asked Randy.

"Maybe we'd better grab some sleep first," Longarm suggested, "then leave early enough to reach the Diamond T first thing in the morning. How many riders do you think might join us, Clem?"

"All of them," replied Hardin emphatically.

"Good. You tell them I'll deputize them. Make it legal."

Hardin nodded. "All right. Get some sleep. I'll go tell the men."

A moment later, as the housekeeper showed Stella to an upstairs bedroom, Stella turned to him and raised her eyebrows questioningly. He grinned and shook his head. Stella laughed and disappeared up the stairs.

She seemed as relieved as he was, Longarm thought to himself wryly.

Chapter 11

Jim Mullin stood on his porch, one hand clutching a post, Pete Davis at his side. Before him, still on their horses, were the two Diamond T riders who had been left with Gulch at the hotel. They had just ridden in, and what they now told Mullin filled him with bitter frustration.

"Both of them dead, you say?"

"That's right," replied the nearest rider. "Gulch and Collins. They was both up there on the second floor. Gulch had the back of his head blowed out, and Collins was alive, just barely. He's the one said it was that deputy marshal."

"And you lost them?"

"It was dark, Mr. Paxman. And there weren't no

tracks to follow. They must've gone through the hills back of town."

"Damn you! Both of you!"

"Sorry, boss," said the other one, "but we done our best."

"Your best!" Mullin cried, his voice choking with fury. "Get out of here! Go on back to the bunkhouse. I'll need you tomorrow."

Both men nodded wordlessly, turned their horses away from the porch, and headed toward the bunkhouse.

"Take me inside," Mullin told Davis. "To my office."

"Ain't you goin' to get any sleep?"

"That's my business!" Mullin snapped.

"Sure, Mr. Paxman."

"And don't call me that any more. The goddamn cat's out of the bag now. My name's Jim Mullin, and I'm all that's left of the Mullin Gang." He said this last with more than a tinge of despair.

As Pete Davis opened the door for Mullin and led him over to his desk, he asked if the boss would be wanting him any more this night.

"No," Mullin said. "Get some sleep. You and I will be moving out tomorrow. Just you and me. I'll need someone like you."

"I might have other ideas, Mr. Mullin."

Mullin grinned slyly. "I should hope so. But I got a sweetener for you—more than twenty thousand dollars."

"You're right, that's a sweetener."

"Good. Get some sleep, but stay close. There's no telling what that son of a bitch marshal will do next."

"Sure, Mr. Mullin."

"You can call me Jim."

"All right, Jim. I'll stay close by."

Mullin nodded, his blind eyes following the big man as he moved out of his office and pulled the door quietly shut behind him. The window by his desk was open and Mullin tipped his head back and listened intently as Pete Davis walked toward the bunkhouse.

It was all coming apart. Benton was probably dead. Swenson was laid up with a broken arm. Those two who had just ridden in and four other riders, none of whom he knew very well, were all that was left of his small army . . . and all because he didn't take care of Loman when he first started to come apart. Mullin realized now that he should never have let him marry that widow. No married man could keep a secret.

But all that was behind him now. He reached down, opened the last drawer in his desk, and pulled out a metal box. The small padlock rattled some as he lifted the box up onto his desk. The key to the lock was in another drawer. His fingers moved swiftly, found the key, and inserted it into the lock. Lifting the lid, he reached in and pulled out the U. S. government's silver certificates. The paper money rustled richly as he flipped its edges with his fingers. It was all still there. He put the money back, locked the box, and placed it back in the bottom drawer.

Then he pulled his gun and holster out and placed it on the top of his desk and waited. He was not at all tired. And, night or day, it was all the same to him.

As dawn broke over the fields ahead of him, Longarm saw the Diamond T's large, two-story log ranch house set in among gently rolling hills pushing out of the morning mists above him. Hardin and Randy Walls were leading three riders around to the rear of the compound, and Longarm judged they were now in position, ready to move in.

He kept his mount to a steady trot and was in the middle of the field when a rifle cracked to his right. Longarm saw a rider bearing down on him. Longarm lifted his horse to a gallop and withdrew his Winchester from its scabbard. At that moment the sound of gunfire came dimly from the hills in back of the bunkhouse. At almost the same moment he saw a hand hurrying toward the ranchhouse leading two saddled mounts.

Longarm turned his horse to meet the rider bearing down on him. With one quick twist he secured the reins to his saddlehorn, lifted the Winchester to his shoulder, and sighted. Just as Longarm squeezed off the shot, his horse swerved to avoid a gopher hole and the round went wild.

Longarm levered a fresh round into the firing chamber and flung up his rifle a second time. The oncoming rider fired again. The round whipped past Longarm like an angry hornet. Standing straight up in his stirrups, Longarm sighted a second time and fired. This time the rider peeled backward off his horse and vanished into the deep grass.

Two more riders, outlined clearly in the bright morning light, made themselves known as they galloped down on him from the left. Both had sixguns in their hands and were firing at him rapidly. Slapping his Winchester back into its scabbard, Longarm snatched his reins and cut away from the two riders, heading for a small gully to his right.

He dug his spurs into his mount and the big chestnut responded magnificently, swiftly lengthening the distance between himself and his two pursuers. As soon as he plunged down into the gully, Longarm cut sharply to his left, then flung himself from his horse, levering a fresh round into his Winchester as he ran. He was crouching behind a boulder when his two pursuers topped the small ridge, both of them clearly outlined in the bright morning's sunlit mist. Longarm sighted on the closest rider and squeezed off a shot. The rider grabbed at his saddlehorn with both hands, then pitched forward over his horse's neck and rolled headfirst into the gully.

His companion pulled up hastily, his horse rearing. Hanging onto the plunging mount, the rider managed to wheel it quickly around. As Longarm threw a round after him, the rider disappeared back the way he had come. Longarm moved out from behind the boulder and listened to the gradual fading of the fleeing horseman's pounding hoofs. The Diamond T rider had evidently had his belly full. One less gunslick to worry about.

Longarm caught his mount's reins and swung into the saddle. The horse was trembling, its flanks quivering. The animal had gone a long way this morning and had just given him the edge he needed. Longarm patted its sweat-dampened neck and urged it up out of the gully. The sound of desultory gunfire came from the bunkhouse and the ground behind it. Hardin and his men had evidently bottled up the remaining Diamond T riders in their bunkhouse.

And there was nothing now between Longarm and the Diamond T.

Mullin was at his open window, his head turned anxiously, his nose in the air, like a terrified animal attempting to discern the scent of his pursuers. Beside the window stood Davis, who had entered a few minutes earlier, after bringing over two saddled horses.

"Come on, Jim," Davis said. "We'd better get moving. Sounds like an army out there around the bunkhouse. While the boys are pinned down, we can make a break for it."

"Damn it, I can't leave now! It's too soon! What can you see out there? What's happening?"

"That rider is still coming on."

"Pender and Wilson didn't stop him?"

"Pender is down and Wilson has cut and run. The way is open for this rider. He's still coming on."

"Who is he?"

Davis hesitated and leaned close to the blind man, peering past him out the window. "Looks like that marshal," he said, his voice suddenly hard.

"Get him, Davis! Break the son of a bitch in two!"

Mullin could feel the big man straightening. He was obviously trying to decide if he should attempt to stand up to this man. So far, this marshal had proven himself to be a remarkably fierce and deadly opponent.

"In my desk!" Mullin snapped. "There's a box in the bottom drawer. The money's in that box. Half of it is yours if you get this man."

"Where's the key?"

"I'll tell you when you come back."

Davis hesitated.

"Go ahead. Pull the strongbox out. Heft it. See for yourself."

Davis went to the desk. Mullin heard him rattling the drawer as he pulled it out, then the solid clunk of the steel box as he set it down on the top of his desk.

"It's in there, Davis. All of it. Twenty thousand dollars. But it won't be worth a pinch of coon shit if we let that son of a bitch out there ride in here and take us."

Mullin heard Davis lifting the box off the desk, and then his footsteps heading for the door. Mullin smiled and brought up the sixgun he had tucked into his belt a second before Davis entered the office.

"Hold it right there," Mullin said softly. "This here is a double-action Colt. Maybe I won't get you with the first round, Davis, but I wouldn't be so sure about

171

the second and third. Just put that box back down on the desk. You know my conditions. Stop that son of a bitch out there and half that money is yours."

Mullin heard Davis chuckle meanly. "Okay, Jim," he said softly. "I'll bring the marshal's head in on a platter. I got a score of my own to settle with him."

"Good! Now go do it."

Mullin heard the box come down hard on the desk top, then Davis's rapid steps as he hurried from the office. A moment later, his head turned to the open window, Mullin heard Pete Davis mount up and spur off across the compound.

Longarm was pounding up from the meadow, heading toward the ranch compound, when he saw the big fellow dart out of the ranch house, mount up, and charge toward him. From his size and the way he rode, Longarm had no doubt that this rider was Pete Davis. He felt a sudden, grim satisfaction. This moment had been a long time coming.

He spurred his horse to greater speed as he headed directly for the oncoming Davis. Davis opened up on Longarm with his sixgun. Longarm kept his head down and drew his own Colt. When the two riders were close enough to see clearly the buttons on each other's shirts, Longarm saw Davis's horse begin to waver, as Davis tried to decide in which direction he should go. Longarm had no intention of pulling aside. If he cut to one side or the other, he would be leaving his flank open to Davis.

At the last possible moment, it was Davis who cut

right. Longarm cut left, slapped his horse's flank sharply, and lit past Davis on a straight line to the big house. His way was clear now. He regretted leaving Davis behind, but it was Jim Mullin Longarm wanted now. Pete Davis could wait.

But Davis had a fresh mount and, turning swiftly, he took after Longarm, gaining rapidly. By the time Longarm reached the main gate of the Diamond T compound, his chestnut was laboring and Davis was rapidly overhauling him. As Longarm glanced back, Davis threw a shot after him—then another.

Longarm leaned forward over the chestnut's neck to urge him to greater speed. But his sudden shift of weight was too much for the exhausted horse. He broke stride, then stumbled forward brokenly. He went down, throwing Longarm clear.

But even as he sprawled forward along the ground, Longarm was reaching for his Colt. He rolled swiftly once, then came up on his hands and knees, turned his head, and looked up. Davis was almost on him, charging full tilt. He intended to ride Longarm down, the enormous bulk of horse and rider already less than ten yards from him.

Longarm flung up his Colt and fired. The bullet thudded into the horse's chest. The animal appeared to disintegrate under Davis, spilling the big man almost at Longarm's feet. Davis scrambled free of the thrashing animal and was on his feet in an instant, charging Longarm like a wildcat just released from a sack.

Longarm had no time for finesse. Regaining his

173

feet in time to meet Davis's charge head-on, he clubbed viciously downward with his gun barrel, catching Davis on the crown of his head. Davis rocked back. Longarm stepped closer and struck him again, this time dragging the gun barrel across Davis's face. Davis went down on one knee, snarling in sudden pain, then reached out and managed to catch hold of Longarm's gun hand. Longarm yanked his hand free and fired deliberately into the man.

Davis spun to the ground, scrabbling frantically for his own sixgun. Longarm saw it gleaming on the hard-packed ground beside the now still horse. He strode quickly past Davis and kicked the weapon away.

Despite his gunshot wound in the chest, Davis tried to get up. Longarm looked down at the huge, slowly twisting form of the man who had tried to beat his head to a pulp after murdering Connie Davis. He remembered Connie dying in his arms, her last request that she be buried beside her mother. And Clem Hardin's deep grief as he looked down at his empty coffee cup and held himself together.

Longarm stepped back and kicked Pete Davis in the face and left him twisting on the hard ground, mewling helplessly, his broken face a mask of blood and gristle.

Turning then, Longarm strode toward the ranch house. The rattle of gunfire coming from the bunkhouse was beginning to peter out, he noticed.

Aware that Pete Davis had failed, Jim Mullin turned from the window as he heard the steady, weary tramp of boots approaching the ranch house. He spun his swivel chair up behind his desk and clawed the strongbox back into its drawer. Then he put his sixgun back in the top drawer and left the drawer open enough for him to reach it quickly.

This done, he called loudly to his housekeeper. He heard her padding steps approach his door, heard her turn the knob and push it open. Her remarkable fidelity amazed him, but this was no time to remark on it.

"Get out while you can. I won't be needing you any more," he told her.

The Indian woman said nothing, and only paused for a moment before pulling the door shut and pattering off into the ranch house.

Mullin turned his face toward the door to his office and waited.

Longarm kicked open the ranch house door and walked inside. He saw a large living room to his left, stairs leading up to the second floor straight ahead of him, and a kitchen down the hall ahead of him. To his right there was a door. He turned the knob and pushed it open.

A blind man was sitting at his desk, waiting for him.

Jim Mullin.

"Come in," Mullin told him. "Come right in. You must be that deputy U. S. marshal. Custis Long."

"And you must be Jim Mullin."

"That's right. I want you to know, Long. I ain't going to any prison. That's no place for a blind man."

"Does it make all that much difference?"

"To me it does. I have a lot of money in this desk, Long. It's in the bottom drawer. Two thousand dollars. It's yours if you'll just put me on that horse Davis brought over and let me ride off."

"You wouldn't get far."

"It doesn't matter. I'd be on a horse, not sitting behind this desk, or trapped behind the bars of a jail cell."

"No."

"It ain't much I'm asking, Long."

"It's all over, Mullin. And you're going to jail."

"No, I'm not!" Mullin's hand snaked into the desk drawer and recoiled from it holding a blazing sixgun.

Longarm flung himself to one side as the slug tore into the wall behind him. A picture was shattered, then slid down the wall. Longarm's own sixgun was out, but he could not bring himself to fire back at the blind man standing up behind the desk. Twice more with a fierce, cold deliberation Mullin fired in Longarm's direction.

Ducking low, Longarm crabbed closer to the desk, seeking it for cover. Suddenly Mullin ducked out and around his desk, heading blindly for the door. Longarm scrambled after him. Mullin's sensitive hearing warned him, and he spun about and fired once more at Longarm.

Longarm dove once more for the floor. As he did so, he saw Pete Davis's bloody torso lurching into the doorframe behind Mullin, his battered face scarcely recognizable. Mullin heard the movement, spun, and fired his last two rounds at Davis. The startled, out-raged Davis raised his own gun and fired three times into Mullin. Mullin uttered a sharp cry—whether it was uttered with relief or despair, Longarm would never be sure—then dropped his gun and crumpled to the floor.

Seeing what he had done, Davis flung himself about and staggered out of the house. Longarm scrambled to his feet and followed after him. The big man was hauling himself into the saddle of the horse he had brought for Mullin. From behind him, Longarm heard the rapid hoofbeats of an approaching horse.

Davis somehow managed to turn his horse. As he started to gallop off, out from behind the house swept Clem Hardin. The man took one look at Davis, flung up his sixgun, and fired. He thumbcocked and fired again. Both rounds found their mark.

As Davis slipped backward out of his saddle, Hardin pulled up alongside him and emptied his gun into the slowly twitching remains of the man who had murdered his daughter.

Chapter 12

As Longarm swung easily onto the black, he straightened his hat and smiled down at the three of them. The four remaining members of Jim Mullins' gang were waiting for him in the jail in Dun Creek. Longarm would take them by stage to Bromfield and from there by train to Denver. He was not looking forward to the trip. But Billy Vail's last telegram had made it clear that he wanted Longarm back in Denver. There were some explanations that simply could not be made understandable in a telegram, even in a series of telegrams.

"Thanks for everything, Clem," Longarm said. "And you be sure to give my best to the doc."

"I'll do that, Longarm," Hardin replied. "Just as soon as he dries out."

Longarm laughed and turned his attention to Stella. Content, it seemed, to stay on at the Lazy H, she smiled happily up at him. Her presence as Hardin's guest had not prevented her and Longarm from enjoying each other's company this past week; but Longarm had a feeling that once he left for good, it would take something close to dynamite to pry Stella loose from Clem Hardin and the Lazy H.

Hardin had been big enough to understand how it was between her and Longarm, and was grateful enough for her company to insist on her staying on at the Lazy H until her own ranch house was rebuilt. Longarm could see how that might take a long, long time.

"Goodbye and good luck, Custis," Stella told him. "And thank you. Thank you for everything."

He smiled back at her. "It was my pleasure."

"If you are ever in these parts again, Longarm," Hardin said, "you must visit us. You're welcome any time."

"I'll remember that, Clem."

Randy Walls ambled over. Longarm waited. When Randy reached Longarm, he reached up and shook Longarm's hand.

"Guess you've figured out how to stop outsmartin' yerself," he drawled, grinning up at Longarm.

"I sure as hell hope so," replied Longarm with a smile. "Take care of these two," he told the old cowpoke, "and stay away from hotel lobbies."

"You can bet I will," said Randy.

Longarm nodded to the three of them, touched the brim of his hat to Stella, then wheeled his horse around and rode out.

He did not look back. And he knew he would not look up Clem Hardin if he was ever in this territory again. By that time, he had no doubt, Stella would be Mrs. Hardin. He had just finished extricating himself from a bellyful of trouble caused by consorting with married women and had decided to swear off them completely.

At least until the next time.

Watch for

LONGARM AT FORT RENO

seventy-third novel in the bold
LONGARM series from Jove

coming in January!

LONGARM

Explore the exciting Old West with
one of the men who made it wild!

___07722-4	LONGARM ON THE GREAT DIVIDE #52	$2.50
___08101-9	LONGARM AND THE BUCKSKIN ROGUE #53	$2.50
___07723-2	LONGARM AND THE CALICO KID #54	$2.50
___07545-0	LONGARM AND THE FRENCH ACTRESS #55	$2.50
___08099-3	LONGARM AND THE OUTLAW LAWMAN #56	$2.50
___07859-X	LONGARM AND THE BOUNTY HUNTERS #57	$2.50
___07858-1	LONGARM IN NO MAN'S LAND #58	$2.50
___07886-7	LONGARM AND THE BIG OUTFIT #59	$2.50
___06261-8	LONGARM AND SANTA ANNA'S GOLD #60	$2.50
___06262-6	LONGARM AND THE CUSTER COUNTY WAR #61	$2.50
___08161-2	LONGARM IN VIRGINIA CITY #62	$2.50
___06264-2	LONGARM AND THE JAMES COUNTY WAR #63	$2.50
___06265-0	LONGARM AND THE CATTLE BARON #64	$2.50
___06266-9	LONGARM AND THE STEER SWINDLER #65	$2.50
___06267-7	LONGARM AND THE HANGMAN'S NOOSE #66	$2.50
___06268-5	LONGARM AND THE OMAHA TINHORNS #67	$2.50
___06269-3	LONGARM AND THE DESERT DUCHESS #68	$2.50
___06270-7	LONGARM AND THE PAINTED DESERT #69	$2.50
___06271-5	LONGARM ON THE OGALLALA TRAIL #70	$2.50
___07915-4	LONGARM ON THE ARKANSAS DIVIDE #71	$2.50
___06273-1	LONGARM AND THE BLIND MAN'S VENGEANCE #72	$2.50
___06274-X	LONGARM AT FORT RENO #73	$2.50

Prices may be slightly higher in Canada.

brands on the beef he saw everywhere. Not long after, he caught sight of the ranch.

It was a prosperous, well-kept spread nestled in amongst pine-clad foothills with a towering, jagged mass of mountains serving as a dim backdrop. A generous stream meandered through the pastureland below the knoll upon which the spacious log ranch house had been built. The barns and sheds and smaller outbuildings were set neatly about the compound. The corral fences were all in fine repair, and everywhere Longarm looked he saw deep, lush grass with heavy, tallowed beef grazing contentedly. Clem Hardin did not believe in overgrazing his lands, it appeared. He was not a greedy man.

As Longarm rode toward the main gate, he could not help marvelling at the rich bounty he glimpsed on all sides of him. His nostrils were filled with the sweet scent of clover mixed with the tang of sage, and his eyes beheld a sweep and beauty, a noble spaciousness, that filled him with awe. This sure as hell was pretty country.

It was impossible for him not to compare all this with the narrow, cluttered streets of Denver. In his mind's eye he saw again Denver's smoke-darkened skies, its pervasive stench, the mud-splattered crowds, the dirt and filth everywhere, and Connie Hardin Davis's battered face as she lay in the hallway of his rooming house—and, later, her mean death in a dusty hotel room.

The contrast was as disheartening as it was impossible to understand. How could Connie have left behind this rich land and the life it offered to journey so far, to such a mean city, to find the miserable death she had?

At the same time, Longarm found himself unable to ignore the fact that he was, in a sense, responsible for Connie's death. She had lied to him, yes. She had told him she was unencumbered—a widow. But he had not been inclined to examine too closely her words; and, as Billy Vail had reminded him, it would probably not have made any difference if he had known she was married.

Two collies darted through the gate to announce Longarm's presence. But their barks held no menace, only pleasure, it seemed, at the sight of him riding into their yard, and Longarm had no difficulty keeping his black under control. A couple of ranch hands stepped out of the bunkhouse and watched him ride in. Another hand left off messing with a bronc in one of the corrals back of the horse barn and climbed the corral rails to look him over also. Halfway to the ranch house, Longarm glanced over and saw Randy Walls, a pitchfork in his hand, step out of the barn, take one startled look at him, and pull up. He looked as if he were seeing a ghost.

Longarm waved to him, then continued on to the hitch rail in front of the ranch house and dismounted. The door to the ranch house opened and a tall, white-haired fellow paused in the doorway. He was blocky in build and powerful in the shoulders and neck. He wore black pants, a white shirt with a black string tie, and a black vest. He was obviously still in mourning.